The Sévigné Letters

A novel by

William Eisner

BASKERVILLE
PUBLISHERS, INC.
DALLAS • NEW YORK • DUBLIN

BASKERVILLE Publishers, Inc.
7616 LBJ Freeway, Suite 220, Dallas, TX 75251-1008

Library of Congress Cataloging-in Publication Data

Eisner, William
      The Sévigné letters / William Eisner.
          p. cm
   ISBN No. 1-880909-27-8 : $18.00 ($25 Canada)
   1. Title
  PS3555.I89S48 1994
  813'.54--dc20   94-30480
                                                             CIP

Manufactured in the United States of America
First Printing, 1994

For Leti

"The prologues are over. It is a question, now,
Of final belief. So, say that final belief
Must be a fiction. It is time to choose."

Wallace Stevens (1879 - 1955)
Asides on the Oboe

1

I could always tell when Mme Colmar wanted to chat. It was usually late afternoon, yellow light fading in the window. There was movement in the hall and a rustling against my door and sometimes a tentative knock and the words, *"Tout va bien, Monsieur Rébair?"* Her hair, parted in the center and pulled back to a knot at the nape of her neck, lay against the sides of her head like folded grey wings. She would invite me to join her in the *salon;* I always accommodated her. To reach her living room we passed through a narrow corridor and skirted a credenza that carried the phone. Mme Colmar was thin, small-boned, erect; as she preceded me down the hall, I had the impression that she had jettisoned all excess bodily baggage on the final leg of a long and ever more difficult journey. She offered me Cointreau served in a cognac glass then sat opposite me: her eyes were extraordinarily bright and sunk in dark hollows, skin drawn taut over salient cheekbones. The incongruous feature was her mouth: it was surprisingly full and carnal. I was twenty-five at the time and to me Mme Colmar seemed impossibly old; I could not begin to guess her age.

Madame's living room contained a sofa in faded blue where she always placed herself, two matching pink and gold stuffed chairs (I learned to choose the one on the left because Mme Colmar's hearing was better in her right ear), and dusty draperies in the same color as the sofa. A coffee table covered with grey lace rested between us, a battered rolltop desk with bowed legs and paws for feet sat below the window, a row of bookshelves along a wall. The carpet was threadbare, fragments of a hunting scene discernible in the fabric. The draperies were always drawn and the only illumination was a dim lamp on a table beside the sofa and close to Madame. I recall an odor of dust and old meals and stale air, street noises barely audible; I think of it now as a crypt, time stopped. It was impossible to conceive that this shabby apartment, which chance had led me to, contained one of the great treasures of France, or that this treasure would create the most profound crisis of my life, a crisis that would reverberate through the years and, like the curse on the ancient mariner, brand me forever.

"What do you write about?" Mme Colmar asks as she sips her Cointreau.

"About the life I've lived and the people I've known," I reply.

"But you're so young, Monsieur Rébair, and have lived so little." She fixes me with a bright stare. "Most young men scribble endlessly about their first love affair and the first time they slept with a woman, as though they have made some brilliant new discovery." I feel guilty since this is exactly what I am writing about: a splendid romance and a failed marriage.

Mme Colmar speaks no English and we converse in French. Mine is halting, the product of three years study in high school and two in college. One of the reasons I chat with her, I tell myself, is to learn the language, but I'm not unhappy to get away from my desk and, besides, I find her company pleasant enough. In one of our first conversations she told me she was particularly pleased that day; she had dreamt of fish the previous night and said this forecasts good luck as fish are a symbol of life. She was certain the dream had something to do with my arrival.

"Your great general has done well," Madame says, pointing to the cover of *Paris-Match* beside her. The caption reads: "MacArthur Returns in Triumph to Seoul, City Recaptured One Month after Fall." MacArthur is wearing his old crushed hat and khakis; Syngman Rhee, a head shorter, stiff and looking both determined and uncomfortable, is beside him. The city in the background is in ruins. "France could use him in Indochina," she says, "where we replace one general with another as often as women change hats." She thinks a minute then adds, "I suspect it makes no difference who the general there is. Napoleon himself would not make a difference."

I left the U.S. two weeks after MacArthur's landing at Inchon and on the last day of the baseball season, when the Phillies beat the Dodgers to win their first pennant in thirty-five years. I wasn't much interested in the World Series; Boston, which was only a couple of games out of first place when MacArthur hit the beach, finished third, behind the Yankees and Detroit, disappointing me once again. When I reached Paris and noticed a photograph on the cover of a French magazine of North Koreans raising their hands in the air and others stripping their officers naked, I thought the war would be over by Christmas. So much for me as a military analyst.

While Mme Colmar and I converse her husband sometimes wanders by. He wears a bathrobe of indefinite color, as old and shabby as the rug; he's badly in need of a haircut, his beard yellow-white and poorly trimmed. He always looks lost; an odor of stale urine trails behind him.

"He was a professor of mathematics," Madame said when he first appeared, nodding her head toward the passing shadow, "and had a theorem named after him when he was only twenty-seven. That was the high point of his life." She gestured toward a photograph on the wall. "That's the great mathematician Henri Poincaré, and it's autographed to my husband. 'To M. Gustave Colmar,'" she said, quoting the dedication from memory, "'for whom a great future awaits.'" It was impossible, even if you were weak in French, to miss the irony in her voice. "He taught in a *lycée* for most of his life. There was no great future. He now suffers from senile dementia." Madame did not appear especially saddened by her husband's state.

Those were her last words with respect to M. Colmar; she paid no further attention to him and after a while I learned as well to ignore his ghost-like presence.

"To write well you must read," Mme Colmar instructs me as we sip Cointreau. I can see that in her search for common ground she has decided to interest herself in my writing. "Read the great ones—Balzac, Stendhal, Flaubert— see how well they construct their characters, men and women built only of words yet more vital and alive than most of the flesh and blood people you know. Read the plays of Racine, the fables of La Fontaine, the poetry of de Musset, Baudelaire, Mallarmé, Apollinaire."

I'm about to comment that other than having read *Madame Bovary* and *Candide* in translation and struggled with Daudet's *Lettres de Mon Moulin* and Balzac's *Le Curé de Tours* in college, my knowledge of French literature is meager, when Madame jumps to her feet, strides to the bookshelves, hunts around, and returns with a thin volume. "Here, let us start with something dramatic. This is Racine's *Bérénice*, a psychological study of a ruler caught between the demands of his position as Emperor of Rome and his love for the beautiful Bérénice."

And Madame proceeds to read Racine's heroic verse, though "read" is a pale word for what she does. Rather Mme Colmar leaps from character to character, vaults in an instant from a tone of imperious command to the unctuousness of a courtier. She raises her eyes: they're bright with the power of Racine. "Do not translate," she cautions, "rather try to 'feel' both the rhythm and the thought of the original."

What she suggests is not easy and I don't try very hard. Instead the scene itself—her face lit only by the golden light of the lamp, all else in shadow—takes on the quality of a Rembrandt painting and settles pleasurably into my being. I sit at the edge of the shadows, not really listening, but drifting as though enchanted. The Cointreau helps.

"There is another great French writer you must read," Mme Colmar says, "and that is Mme de Sévigné. We know her only through her letters, mostly written to her daughter—who did not merit the treasure of words her mother heaped upon her. Mme de Sévigné and her most intimate friend, the novelist Mme de La Fayette, were the two greatest women of the 17th century." I don't suppose it ever occurred to Madame to add the qualifier "French" in front of "women."

"Read de Sévigné," Madame insists. "Read her for the direct, immediate way she describes the world, reality as we actually experience it, undistorted by analysis or explanation. She is the finest chronicler of France's greatest century."

Madame smiles, touches my sleeve. "Here," she says, once again striding to the bookshelves. "I have all the collected letters of Mme de Sévigné in these volumes." She runs her hand across at least a dozen books then takes one and hands it to me. "Read this one. It is my favorite." The brown leather cover is discolored, cracked, the title, *Grands Ecrivains de France*, in gold, barely visible. I carefully open the book: it's dated 1864, the paper yellowed at the edges, brittle. For some reason I expect the mummified remains of a pressed flower to drop from between the pages. I think of ancient chronicles—*Beowulf, The Canterbury Tales, King Arthur*—and thank her for the book. I'm certain I will never read it.

It would take some time for me to learn how deeply Mme Colmar related to de Sévigné and the central role that 17th century writer's letters would play in my life.

As our conversations progressed, the Cointreau, the effort of following Madame's French, the weak illumination, perhaps the lack of oxygen, had a lulling effect, and I relaxed, a kind of voluptuous relaxing, and now as I reconstruct those times, I'm no longer sure what was truly said versus what I imagine was said. I do remember that when I spoke Madame's gaze stayed fixed on my face, an indulgent look, and I could usually tell when my French went awry because her eyes would crinkle, though she rarely corrected me. Now I think of her face as a reflection of my own, and in contemplating her, I am contemplating myself.

"Our problem," Lea says as she sips her *café filtre* and morosely stares out into the Paris night, "is that we're poor." We're at the Café Odéon on the Boulevard St. Germain, the place pleasantly warm after the damp chill outside.

"That's true," I reply, "but I don't feel particularly deprived. I should have my book finished by the time my GI Bill money runs out, then I'll go home. I don't live much worse here than I did in the States."

"Are you people American?" the man at the adjacent table asks. He's older than we, blond with rimless glasses and a professional look. He's also the only person in the place wearing a business suit and tie. A lonely tourist out of season.

"Did you just get here?" I ask.

"Three days ago. This is just a stopover. I'm a doctor on my way to Zurich to study leukemia. With all the radiation we and the Russians are letting loose in the air, that's the up and coming disease." He speaks in a horn-like voice, a man used to giving lectures.

"Is that right?" I say politely.

The doctor takes this as a serious challenge. "Absolutely. Look at Hiroshima. The area around it has ten times more leukemia than the rest of Japan. Believe me, it's the disease of the future. And the Swiss know a hell of a lot more about it than we do." He looks us over. "Are you people students?"

"We both attend the Sorbonne," Lea says. "On and off, you might say."

"But you're French, aren't you?" the doctor says to Lea. "Your accent is French with a hint of English... I love a French accent." Lea stares past the doctor and across the avenue: on a pedestal, illuminated by the streetlamps, a bronze Danton has his right arm decisively extended and pointing down the boulevard as though he's directing traffic. "You know," the doctor says, focusing first on Lea's bored face then on me, "I was about to go to dinner. Would you people care to join me?" We both hesitate. "It's on me," he quickly adds. He checks the guidebook beside him. "There's a place nearby called Le Procope. It's the oldest restaurant in the city." The book seems to take on a fascination for him; he reads in schoolteacher fashion: "Voltaire, Benjamin Franklin, Napoleon and Balzac were among its clients. The restaurant was founded by—"

7

Lea stands up. "Shall we go?" she says. The doctor leaps to his feet.

"My name is Vernon, Michael C. Vernon," he says while sticking his hand out toward me. He's taller than I expected and smells of cologne.

"Frank Reeber," I say.

It's still early when we enter Procope and the place is nearly empty. The maître d', face expressionless, still manages to convey that Lea and I should be using the back door. "Do you have reservations?" he asks in French.

Vernon takes charge in English and we're seated, but in a corner. Lea looks around at the mahogany paneling, burgundy carpet, linen tablecloth and napkins, heavy silverware and I can see her opinion of the doctor rising like a party balloon. I study the menu: it's elaborate and impossibly expensive. My opinion of Dr. Vernon soars alongside of Lea's. I order steak, something I haven't eaten since leaving America, and Lea orders trout. Vernon suggests a bottle of red wine for the meat eaters and a bottle of white for Lea. She says she's not compulsive about these red/white distinctions and red wine would be fine. Vernon orders a bottle of Chateauneuf du Pape and the sommelier, after an anguished rubbing of hands, makes polite noises about the fish. Lea tells him in French that red wine with fish is a new trend; the man listens gravely, resignation in his creased face, then inclines his head and disappears.

"Medicine is in a lousy state in France," Vernon says. "Mostly because they don't have the latest drugs. It's their miserable bureaucracy." He stares at us, face serious; the subject seems important to him. "You can't beat the Latins for bureaucracy. Take drug approval for example. The drug of choice for the treatment of arthritis is cortisone. They've been selling it in Switzerland for almost a year now, but the French haven't approved it and there's no way you can buy cortisone in France." He seems genuinely indignant over the injustice done French arthritis sufferers.

"What exactly is cortisone?" I ask, more out of politeness than real curiosity. My mind is focused on the steak.

"God, where've you been?" Vernon says. "The two guys from the Mayo clinic who just won the Nobel prize in medicine got it for their discovery of the anti-inflammatory effects of cortisone. One of their patients was this twenty-nine year old woman, bedridden and barely able to move. After only a week on cortisone, she was zipping around downtown Rochester on a shopping spree."

"How long do you have to take the stuff?" I ask.

"A couple of months."

"Is it a permanent cure?" Lea asks.

"Nobody is quite sure yet," Vernon says.

"Do the French know something the Swiss don't?" I ask. "Maybe there's some negative side to this cortisone."

"Not at all," Vernon says, professional again. "It's a benign, perfectly natural drug, synthesized by the adrenal glands. Everybody produces a small amount of cortisone, otherwise we'd all be arthritic. Heck, women with arthritis get well during pregnancy, at least temporarily. That's because the adrenal glands put out more hormones during gestation. No, what we have here is French bureaucracy at work."

"A couple of million francs in the right places and any drug would be approved here quick enough," Lea says.

"I think the authorities are waiting for a French company to go into production before giving approval," Vernon says. "They want to keep the market to themselves. It's damned unfair."

I'm bored with the subject, stare at the painting of a bewigged French nobleman on the wall above Vernon's head (the guy seems remote, vaguely discouraged), then try to shift the conversation to the possible U.S. war with China, the anti-American graffiti scrawled on the walls in the Latin Quarter, Connie Mack's retirement from baseball after sixty-seven years in the game, anything, but Vernon always returns to cortisone and the poor suffering arthritics in France. I notice that Vernon has a rectangle disorder: while we wait for our food, he continually arranges and rearranges his silverware, wine and water glasses, salt and pepper shakers, and any other object he can put his hands on, so it is perpendicular to everything else.

The steak is unbelievably good. As I wash down the delicious chunks with the rich thick Chateauneuf du Pape I can feel years being added to my life, chapters to my novel. I'm so involved with the steak that I miss Vernon's proposition. Lea says, "But what sort of commission would you pay?"

I catch up. Vernon has proposed that we act as his agents, that we visit pharmacies in Paris and inquire who is interested in buying cortisone. He would ship the order to them or us, from Switzerland.

"I would pay you twenty percent of the sales price," Vernon says.

"But it's illegal, isn't it?" I observe, not too brilliantly.

"When it comes to healing the sick, nothing is illegal," Vernon says, glasses scintillating and his voice rich with feeling.

"That may be fine theoretically," I say, "but you get thrown in jail if you get caught selling black market drugs... Isn't that right?"

Vernon has a brief silent struggle with this thought then shrugs. "That risk is covered by the twenty percent commission... But I can understand that you might want to think about it." He takes a handsome little notepad, leather-covered, from the breast pocket of his jacket, removes a small gold pen from a slot in the notepad and writes. "Here's my address and phone number in Zurich." He tears out the page and hands it to Lea. "If you're interested, let me know. The drug is sold as an injectable serum in vials, five shots to a vial. I sell the vials at 50,000 francs each, or about $125 a vial... A small price for an arthritis sufferer."

"Sounds awfully steep," I say.

"Only those who suffer can judge the value of relief," Vernon says. He's very serious.

Throughout this exchange Lea watches Vernon. I recognize the look—it's the one that was on her face during our first conversations, at Boston University's student union, when I told her about myself—the look of a jury evaluating a witness.

All that red meat and wine has put much lead in my pencil. "How about going to your room?" I say to Lea after the doctor has disappeared into a cab. I find my voice is husky.

On the way I ask, "What do you think of Vernon?"

"I don't think he's exactly young Lochinvar come out of the west to save the arthritics of France," she says. Lea has a weakness for the Romantic poets, thus far the only weakness I've detected. "But he seems legitimate, an enterprising doctor looking to make an extra franc."

"How do you know he isn't making it all up and won't just ship vials of water?"

Lea waves an impatient hand. "You have to trust your instincts. But even if I'm wrong—and I doubt it—water wouldn't hurt anybody. Anyway, if you *believe* you're going to feel better, then often enough you do."

I decide it's the wrong moment to discuss the morality of selling vials of water at 50,000 francs a pop as a cure for arthritis.

"I like the idea of selling Vernon's cortisone," she continues. "It doesn't sound tough, and getting 10,000 francs for every vial you sell... that's interesting." Lea turns toward me when she says this: she has sea-green eyes flecked with gold.

I have difficulty focusing on the conversation but do my best. "I didn't come to Paris to be a drug salesman," I say. "It'll interfere with my work. And your school for that matter. Besides, winding up in a French jail doesn't appeal to me."

I can see that Lea is getting irritated, a bad humor for what I have in mind. "Don't exaggerate," she says. "There's a black market for everything in France, from drugs to watches to money. If every black marketeer in France were put in prison, there wouldn't be anybody left on the streets. Opportunity has just hammered on our door, and you're saying we should ignore it."

We turn on the Rue Galande, a skinny cobblestone street where the buildings lean toward each other like drunks, and climb four rickety flights to reach Lea's room. The place is furnished with a bed, a desk, a small table and a closet, all on a mud-colored wood floor. To wash, she has to get water from the bathroom down the hall. I pull her toward the bed. "Listen," she says, her breath warm and moist against my mouth, "do we do this pharmacy thing or not?" At that moment I would have agreed to anything.

"I think I know what the 'C' in Michael C. Vernon stands for," I say as we entwine on her bed.

"Cortisone?" Lea ventures, stealing my line.

2

"I consulted my
tarot reader this morning," Mme Colmar tells me, "and the
first card in the sequence was an ace." She seems in
excellent spirits.

"Is that important?" I try to suppress a smile.

"Do not laugh," Madame says, face suddenly grave.
"The tarot is like a great book, written in a symbolic
language akin to Egyptian hieroglyphics, that one opens at
random. In it are all the materials from which our lives are
formed. One need only read and interpret."

"The ace?" I ask.

"It signifies beginning, possibility, change... Actually,
there were two aces, which makes the point stronger yet."

"What did the cards say?" I feel I'm being thrust back to
some medieval time, but then much of the city gives me that
impression. When I arrived, I found a room in a rundown
hotel on the Rue Cardinal Lemoine; I dropped my old Army

13

Air Force B-4 bag on the floor and stared out the window at the streaked buildings and the forest of chimney pots, wisps of smoke rising toward a pewter-colored sky, and experienced a sense of elation. I was certain the scene had not changed in at least a hundred years; I was free of Boston, of America, even my own century.

Madame looks away, as though I'm probing into a secret and shameful thought. "Much of it is mine alone and I can't reveal it. But there was the wheel, the hermit, and the moon, the ace of wands and the two of cups." She makes a small gesture with her hands. "All these together signify both large and small things."

"At least tell me the small things."

She gives me an impish look. "I must absolutely dine out this evening. That's one small thing... Shall we dine to-gether?"

"I would be delighted," I say. "But we can do that whether the tarot suggests it or not. I'm afraid I don't much believe in fortunetelling."

"But isn't there divining in your own life? Haven't you ever had a feeling, a premonition?"

"Yes, and most of the time it's wrong... But tell me, if all your future is predetermined, and readable in the cards, doesn't that make life rather dull? Doesn't a life in which all is known in advance lose the charm of being lived?"

Madame smiles and nods in approval. "That's very clever, *jeune homme*. There are indeed shadowy regions, a certain mystery not revealed, otherwise we would have neither hope nor desire."

At that moment I feel a tenderness toward Madame: she is both innocent and wise, otherworldly and practical, and this coexistance of opposites is new to me. I'm struggling for words to express this when she says, "Cards aside, it's important to go out into the world... You know, there used to be a church in Paris called the Church of the Innocents.

Women who wanted to retire from the world or who, for some reason, were forced to retire, were given a cell there. Each cell was then walled shut leaving only a small aperture through which she could view a portion of the church and a cemetery and through which food was pushed each day. Once in, she stayed for life. One woman stayed for forty-six years. Another entered when she was eighteen and remained entombed until her death at the age of ninety-eight." Mme Colmar gestures at the walls around us. "I must avoid this place becoming my Church of the Innocents." At that moment her husband wanders into the room, looks around in his usual confused way, then wanders out. The odor of stagnant urine remains.

She takes me to dinner at the Brasserie Balzar, on the Rue des Ecoles, and holds my arm as we walk along the Boulevard St. Michel toward the restaurant. People hurry by. "Everyone rushes so," Madame says. "It must become a habit. Even if they are returning to an empty room, they rush."

The Balzar is several cuts below Procope, but I'm impressed all the same. Madame wears a dark blue dress; a blue and gold silk scarf covers her throat. She studies the menu with great seriousness. I check the right side of the menu and become apprehensive; perhaps I misunderstood and she expects me to pay. I can't reconcile her modest apartment and taking in a boarder with the restaurant.

"Do you have any children?" I ask.

"One daughter. Our son died many years ago—on August third, nineteen-fourteen, to be precise—the day Germany declared war on France. We were on holiday at Honfleur when he died, a boy of twelve, in a drowning accident."

"I'm so sorry."

She raises her shoulders in a fatalistic gesture that I have seen Lea's parents make many times. "I came to accept this years ago, as the will of Providence, although my husband never did. His life darkened after that and he was never again the same. Much later, when asked about the boy, he would say the lad died in the war."

"And your daughter?"

Madame's manner becomes brusque. "She lives in Orléans, unmarried and now of a certain age... runs a small business, making custom gowns and formal women's wear... quite successful, really." She thinks a moment. "What she really does is copy the designs of the great Parisian couturiers and sell them at a reduced price."

I find the level of contempt in Madame's voice out of scale with her daughter's transgression, and sense a well-spring of bitterness that makes me uncomfortable. I'm about to change the subject when Madame completes her study of the menu and says, "Have you ever eaten lobster?"

Of course, living in Boston, I've eaten lobster many times, but I can see what answer will make her happy. "No, I never have," I say.

She smiles and touches my hand—a warm touch; for some reason I had expected her fingers to be glacial. "Then you shall have a real treat." And she orders lobster and a bottle of Pouilly-Fuissé for us both.

"Have you had a chance to read any of Mme de Sévigné's letters?"

"Just a little," I lie further. "She's most interesting." Actually I did try one night before falling asleep, but I had difficulty with the archaic 17th century French spelling. There was something else: as I held the book an odor of dust and crumbling paper rose from the pages and I had a confused sense of age and decay, then I thought of death, a grey suffocating presence in the room, and hastily set the book down.

"You know," Mme Colmar says, "speaking of Mme de Sévigné—" I thought she was once again going to tell me what a fine writer de Sévigné was, but instead she says, "—it's remarkable how closely our lives parallel... We were both born on the same day and month of the year, were both an only child, and both of us were orphaned by the age of seven and raised by our grandparents. And as if that were not enough, we both married when we were eighteen, had our first child a year later, a girl, and our second and last child, a boy, two years after that." She stares into the void for a moment. "I think I will die on the same day as Madame de Sévigné." She stares a moment longer then moves her hand rapidly, as though waving away a persistent insect.

"I read in the newspaper that your playwright George Bernard Shaw has died," she says. "A very sentimental man apparently. He asked that his ashes be mixed with those of his wife. It's so American: barbaric yet touching all the same."

"He's English, actually Irish, not American," I say, and realize I'm being pedantic; it's no doubt all the same to Madame, holed up in her Church of the Innocents. "You would like his work, particularly *Saint Joan*." I try, with some difficulty, using too many verbs and screwed up subjunctives, to explain why. In an attempt to appear erudite I quote Shaw's famous line, the image of the poor women alone forever in their cells still in my mind, "Silence is the most perfect expression of scorn."

"Then my husband must scorn the world completely," Madame says. "He has not spoken a word in five years. But even when he did speak, he said little, severed by his equations from life." But her eyes sparkle and she doesn't appear at all dispirited by the silence of her husband. She touches my hand again. "How is the lobster?" she asks. Her cheeks are flushed; I attribute this to the Pouilly-Fuissé.

I find the meat tough compared to Boston lobster. "It's superb," I say.

Two couples take a nearby table; one of the women, roughly Mme Colmar's age, places a box about the size of a cigarette pack in the center of the table; a wire, like an errant nerve, runs from her ear to the box. A man yells into the box a story of two policemen commenting on a passing helicopter. "*Voilà une hélicoptère,*" says one. "*Non, non,*" says the other. "It's *un hélicoptère.*" The first cop squints up at the chopper and exclaims, "But you have extraordinary eyesight!" Everyone at the table finds this hilarious, the woman with the hearing aid most of all; she throws her head back and laughs, or rather shrieks, mouth wide open. Madame watches and never cracks a smile. "To be reduced to a box on the table," she says. "Better off dead. At least one retains one's dignity."

When the check arrives, Madame slips money into my hand.

She takes my arm as we stroll home and under her breath sings *La Vie en Rose.* Frost has blackened the flowers in the garden in front of the Musée de Cluny; on the granite wall of Barclay's Bank someone has painted in scrawly black Yankee Go Home—a clear case of mistaken identity. We pass the bronze statue of Montaigne: arms folded, legs crossed, he looks out from above his ruffed collar with a benevolent smile. Madame lightly touches his protruding shoe, shiny from other touches. "It brings good fortune," she says.

"That was a delightful evening," Madame says when we are in the apartment. She stands on her toes in the dim light of the corridor and kisses me on the lips, then to my surprise slips her tongue in my mouth. "Good night," she whispers, then disappears as hurriedly as a schoolgirl.

As I prepare for bed, Madame's kiss stays with me. And she herself changes: no longer is she an interesting if eccentric old lady, but a woman, and I find that I'm sizing her up as a woman. The sense of voluptuous relaxing that settled on me as we sipped Cointreau and conversed now takes on a less innocent meaning, something that both attracts and repels me.

October 17. As soon as the young man sat before me, hands folded respectfully in his lap, light-brown eyes intent as he followed my French, I knew he was the one. I even lowered the rent to be certain he would accept. There must be a secret transaction that takes place between people, some mysterious exchange of sympathies that says yes, yes, we can know each other.

October 26. I thought we would have little to say, but quite the opposite is true. I babble anything that comes into my head, and he listens, brow knitted; occasionally he nods in understanding. Perhaps he does not comprehend everything but that he listens and tries is satisfaction enough. I can see that sometimes the French fatigues him, his eyes dim and he gazes beyond me. I then ask him about America and his work. The tale he writes is so transparently autobiographical that it is touching, and he relates it all in a French that is charmingly simple and full of errors. I suppose one lives three times: in anticipation, in the moment, then in reminiscence, each time differently and often with increasing disappointment. He is facing his broken affair as he writes of it, trying to determine where it failed, ascribing blame, and I suspect, like all of us, distorting the circumstance to his advantage. He is being as much formed by the writing of his book as the book is formed by him… He has splendid hands, slender and innocent, smooth-skinned, with long sensitive fingers. I keep resisting the urge to take his hand. Occasionally I cannot refrain and lightly touch his flesh. The shock causes a delicious shiver to run through me, as though some profound and exquisite communication has taken place.

November 1. I visited with Mme Parlanges yesterday

afternoon and told her of the young man. She, in her questioning way, asked me whether he wanted anything. "I have the impression," I said, "that he wishes to be protected."

"Protected from what?" she asked.

"From life, I suppose."

"It will finish badly," she concluded. "But I have told you this before and my words have never deterred you so I do not believe they will now."

It is not true that these things have always finished badly, though they have always finished. But disaster is so ingrained in poor Mme Parlanges that if she said things will work out well, I would have swooned with disbelief.

November 4. The tarot reading earlier this morning gave me great satisfaction. I hesitate to write what the cards revealed. To put it into words would diminish the anticipation.

November 5. I have complained to the young man of Berthe. I must not do this. She is my burden, not his, and he seemed uncomfortable at my grumbling. It is difficult for an outsider to comprehend my dislike for her. It is difficult for me. The sight of her, her voice on the telephone, never fail to irritate me. I suppose I should be grateful for what she does for us, but experience only disdain.

We have kissed, or rather I kissed him. There in the corridor I could detect the scent of his body, discern the arc of his lips, and could not contain myself. He was surprised and it was with reluctance that I hurried away. I have never been able to hide passion, to disguise it in some other form, the way I am it cannot help but emerge.

The pharmacist wears a white coat and appears as neat and antiseptic as the boxes and tubes and flasks on display in the store. One wall is covered by row on row of porcelain jars, ivory-colored, each ornamented with a floral pattern and words in an elaborate script that I cannot read. The whole display is labeled *herboristerie*. I imagine elves prowling the forest primeval in search of these exotic ingredients. I wonder what maladies they cure but it seems like the wrong moment to ask. The pharmacist's smooth face and noncommittal blue eyes seem thoroughly scrubbed and sterilized as he stares at Lea. The place has a medicinal smell, reminding me of fever, perspiration, misery. I'd like to leave, forget the whole thing.

"It's a corticosteroid," Lea says, apparently having read up on the subject, "identical to that produced by your own adrenal glands. In America, where the beneficial effects of the drug were discovered, patients suffering from arthritis enter the hospital in a wheelchair and in a week are dancing in the wards. It's a miracle." I hardly recognize Lea when she speaks French; there is a change in gesture, manner, an ease and confidence take over and I find her captivating. She bears down on the word "miracle." I don't see how the pharmacist can resist.

"Does this function for both rheumatoid and osteo-arthritis?" the druggist asks, his expression unchanged.

"Rheumatoid," Lea answers without hesitation. "The most terrible because it cripples young people, even children, those with their lives still before them."

I wonder whether Lea isn't in the wrong line of work. She speaks of cortisone as though she has been on intimate terms with the drug all her life. That she labored for a year over a master's thesis on Proust and is fixated on an advanced degree, I decide, must reflect the imprint of her family: something tattooed onto her mind—the Jewish emphasis on learning and her father's preoccupation with things literary—rather than any natural inclination.

"The drug has not been approved by the French authorities," the pharmacist says.

"It's used in America," Lea says, "the most cautious of

21

countries for medication. And it's used in Switzerland. You'll be doing your clients a great service."

"How much?"

"A hundred thousand francs for a vial containing five injections," she says, doubling Michael Vernon's price.

The pharmacist stares at her. "You're insane," he says. "You're wasting my time. Good day." And he turns and disappears into the rear of his store.

"The relief of suffering is priceless," Lea calls after him.

"Try aspirin," he calls back.

"*Merde!*" Lea says when we are on the street. The word for her seems to more graphically convey the notion of "shit" than the English equivalent.

"I think we've established that a hundred thousand francs is too high," I observe.

We try other pharmacies. I'm amazed to find that Paris is full of pharmacies. Their illuminated green crosses are everywhere, their display windows filled with advertisements for potions that fix your liver, smooth your skin, adjust your bowels. I loiter at one window where a gigantic vase in the form of a top and filled with a blue liquid hangs on a chain from the ceiling. I ask Lea what she thinks it is; she gives the affair an impatient glance, shrugs and heads inside without answering. Some druggists won't talk to us at all. One man who has the stern face of Louis Pasteur, throws us out. But some listen and a few say—after Lea has dropped her price—that they'll query their clients.

"This is going to work out fine," Lea says. "Ten thousand francs commission per vial. We could eat for weeks on a single vial."

"We've wasted three days," I say. "You haven't gone to school and I haven't worked on my book. We've talked to maybe fifty pharmacists and all we've gotten are a couple of maybes. The whole thing is ridiculous."

"It's more than a couple," Lea says. "Besides, the first

olive out of the jar is always the toughest... Why don't you follow up with Blithe Spirit, that sweet bird man on the Rue Cluny. I'll handle the rest."

I'm overcome by the way her lips pucker on the u sound in Rue and Cluny and as I kiss her I discover, mingled with the warm pressure of Lea's mouth, greed within myself.

"All right," I say. "I'll follow up with Blithe Spirit but that's it."

3

I work on my
novel. I write in a child's composition notebook that has a
mottled black and white cover and while I struggle with
what to write next I doodle in the margins. Some margins
are filled with doodles that spill over, invade the rest of the
page (they're mostly geometric things—cones piercing pyra-
mids, spheres with pieces cut out—sometimes perched atop
fanciful smiling animals), and seem more important than
the story. At times I stare at the wall in front of my desk—
a faded print in a narrow wooden frame of a Daumier pen
and ink courtroom sketch stares back at me—and struggle
to find the center of my book. I know it must have a center
because the book is me and if it doesn't have a center then
I don't either and that's unthinkable. Now and then I hit an
inspired stretch and scribble page after page, more often I
cross out a lot and I'm back to doodling and staring.
Sometimes I take a break and pace my cell of a room then

stop to gaze out the window at the bleak dead garden and the scrawny leafless tree in the center. I recall Madame's comment on the practice of any profession in Paris: "In every *métier*, from the carpenter to the writer, to settle in Paris is to find oneself among the chosen, the ennobled." But I don't feel myself particularly chosen and I ask myself whether anyone will ever want to read this nonsense.

Occasionally the radiator of the central heating system makes a brief hissing sound, like air going out of a balloon, and is lukewarm for a while, but most of the time it's the coldest object in the room. So I sit at my desk, wearing two sweaters and a scarf, and for internal fuel munch on chocolate that I buy in great chunks from a *confiserie* on the Rue St. Jacques; I leave the chocolate on my dresser. The room is now damp. To economize, all my clothes are drip-dry; I wash them in my sink and hang them on cords that I've rigged across the room. Madame ignores this. Most of the time the water is cold. Each morning Madame leaves a kettle of hot water outside my door for me both to wash with and make tea, half a *baguette* of bread, a chunk of butter and a dollop of jam in a saucer.

Some days I attend the Sorbonne; I'm enrolled in their Course in Civilization, a combination of French history, literature, art and language, as though all of civilization were contained in France. I don't really have to go, no one takes attendance and, unlike Lea, I have no interest in an advanced degree. My monthly GI Bill check will arrive at the American Embassy whether I show up at the Sorbonne or not. But it's good to get away from my claustrophobic room and claustrophobic novel. The history, literature and art lectures, conducted in a chilly amphitheater by elderly men in grey tweed jackets over grey sweaters whose voices are absolutely without inflection, put me into a stupor. I have the impression that this drone has been going on since the beginning of time. The place smells of body odor and damp. I never bother with the assigned reading and try to ignore those around me scribbling in notebooks. At times a shaft of sunlight slants through the window and illuminates a corner of the room; I gaze at the flickering dust motes and think how refreshing it would be if a miracle occurred there.

The language class is a bouillabaisse of nationalities, many of the students Arab, and the instructor a small-eyed dumpy woman. She speaks precisely, words rounded, perfectly shaped, like eggs. I suppose the language class is worthwhile but then I find myself mesmerized by the jiggle of the instructor's rump, as though it were filled with gelatin, as she scrawls verb conjugations on the blackboard, and I have to listen to everyone else's lousy accent.

After class I sometimes meet Lea. Once I introduced her to a group of Arabs. I liked the solid way she shook hands all around. Everyone spoke English and we drank beer together; the Arabs had no problem with liquor but they did with Lea. They stared at her with puzzled faces as they wiped beer foam from their mustaches: she dressed casually, wore no makeup, never bothered to flirt, and told them what she thought. They didn't know how to deal with a woman who spoke to them man to man.

I met Lea last spring at Boston University, in the Mugar library. I had raised my head from a page of Laplace transforms and Bode diagrams and sat gazing (I don't know for how long) at an Arthur Goodwin painting of the old Boston custom house when the girl opposite me said, "You look like a troubled man." She must have been watching me, and I, in mourning over the disintegration of my marriage, bored at the electronics company where I was working, demotivated as I labored at night toward a master's in electrical engineering, and up to my clavicle in self-pity, had not noticed. When we left together she said, "So tell me knight-at-arms, what ails thee, alone and palely loitering?" I recognized the Keats and detected her foreign accent, and was charmed by both. We wandered over to the student union and talked for an hour about what ailed me—then I lost my head and blew a chunk of a week's salary on dinner together at Locke-ober's. She introduced me to her literary friends; I listened to their discussions over pizza and beer and was bewitched; I thought they had discovered some wondrous new ordering of human activity whose importance I could only dimly grasp. I decided that these people, intense and committed, were far closer to the heart of things than we poor engineers, toiling over our vacuum tubes and oscilloscopes.

On the radio all that summer the Weavers sang "Good Night Irene," which was awful for me since the girl I had been married to was named Irene. (One of the things that irritated me about my Irene was that after we were married she started to wear beauty patches to work—adhesive bits of black silk in the shape of a quarter moon, a four-leaf clover, or a heart, that she tacked beneath an eye or next to her mouth. She had a job as a bookkeeper in a wholesale plumbing supply house and I didn't see where this kind of ornamentation was at all appropriate. We had a big argument over the patches—which I thought suitable for a whorehouse but not for an establishment that sold toilets— but she kept on wearing them all the same.) The line in "Good Night Irene" that stuck with me was, "Sometimes I take a great notion to jump in the river and drown."

I tried my hand at writing, overwrought stories of failed relationships and dreadful misunderstandings, and proudly showed them to my new friends and to Lea. They all encouraged me but it was Lea I listened to. She seemed to have the best grip on what writing was about, her comments the most perceptive, her encouragement the most meaningful. And when I wrote I wondered what her reaction to a story would be and how best to please her. She

27

was struggling with her Proust thesis at the time, the sixteen worn volumes of the Gallimard edition of his novel scattered over her desk. She had plowed through all those books three times; I would stare at them in disbelief—you had to admire her single-mindedness.

At the end of one bad day I encounter Madame in the corridor and comment, as I slouch against the sturdy oak credenza, "An artist's life is a difficult one." It sounds presumptuous as hell to me, even in French, as I say it.

Madame laughs. "To be your age and have an entire life yet to live, what could be more wonderful?"

"To write and publish a great book would be a good start," I say.

"Life is not arranged for human happiness," Madame says, her voice lighthearted as she leads me to the *salon*. She breaks out the Cointreau but hesitates before pouring. "You look hemmed in, caged. Would you like to take a walk? The weather is decent and it is not yet night."

Mme Colmar wears plain flat shoes, a black cloth coat with a worn grey fur collar, and a black cloche hat that she places at a rakish angle. We cross the Boulevard St. Germain to the Rue de l'Odéon and stroll toward the Luxembourg gardens. Men are dressed in suits and scarves, collars and lapels turned up against the November chill; women wear top coats, usually dark, utilitarian; most everyone appears a bit shabby. On the boulevard there are more bicycles than automobiles. "How splendid to be out," Madame says, taking my arm. "This is the best time, dusk, *entre chien et loup*, when it is no longer day but not yet night."

"Let us cross the street," Madame says as we approach the Luxembourg. She points to the wall of the adjacent building; the stone face is pocked in a horizontal band about five feet from the ground; the holes seem to form a message in Braille. "Those are bullet marks. This is where *les épinards* slaughtered a dozen students in cold blood." I look at her uncomprehending.

"The Germans," she explains. "They wore spinach-green uniforms... This side of the street is cursed and brings misfortune." She launches into the street and I yank her arm in time to keep her from being hit by a bicycle. "Thank you, *chéri*." She squeezes my arm. "You saved my life... I told you this place was cursed."

The Luxembourg is almost empty. Madame pauses to contemplate the Senate building and the octagonal pool. The façade of the building is black with grime but its huge windows, like the pool, reflect the remaining daylight and appear brighter than the sky. The marble statues of the ancient queens of France, on the esplanade around the pool, seem to draw to themselves what light there is and stand out like ghosts in the gathering darkness. Madame's face glows in the failing light. She seems to expand in the cold air and as we move through the garden she kicks the dead leaves underfoot and does a little dance step. "Now and spring are my favorite seasons," she says and takes my arm. "Things change, decline, are renewed. I could never live in Provence. How dull it would be. Trees there never vary, always an endless shade of green." Madame's voice, here in the garden, takes on a youthful lilt; I imagine exclamation points after every sentence.

We walk without speaking; the leafless branches are jumbled like oriental calligraphy against the dim sky. The gas lamps in the park go on and form islands of brightness in the gloom. A bird darts through the light and disappears. "Night isn't simply the negative of day," Madame says. "It's a different beast altogether, a whole new creation... disappearing lines, eclipse, sightlessness... sinister really, foreshadowing peril, disaster." But her voice is without darkness as she says this and as we walk, her face, touched at intervals by the golden light of the lamps, strikes me as happy and surprisingly youthful.

A man approaches. Even in the dim light it is clear that his jacket is in ruins and he's inadequately covered against the cold. "*Bonsoir*," he says and pauses as we come close to him.

"*Bonsoir*," Madame replies and pauses also. The man's hair is thin and the skin of his face like paper that has been crumpled then opened. "Can we help you Monsieur?"

"Only if you can magically cure disease," he says, his voice raspy, oddly muffled, as though forced past an obstruction in his throat.

Madame snaps open her purse and fishes out a 500 franc note. "A decent meal is a start toward curing anything," she says as she extends the money.

"You are most kind, Madame." He bows as he takes the bill then says, "When I saw you approaching, dressed in black, I thought you were death coming for me. You see I imagine my own death all the time. It's a kind of discipline. In that way I'm not afraid of it."

"That's not good," Mme Colmar says. "La Rochefoucauld would tell you that neither the sun nor death can be looked at steadily."

"I'm conscious of every organ of my body," the man continues. "The state of my heart, lungs, liver, spleen, even my teeth." Madame shakes her head. The man stares at her. I'm about to pull her away when he says, "I'm a musician, a clarinetist." He inclines his head at this revelation, a modest smile on his face. "My name is Léon Chantal. Perhaps you were present at my performance of Mozart's clarinet concerto... Before the war. 1938. With maestro Pierre Monteux and the Orchestre Symphonique de Paris... Listen—is there anything more beautiful than this?" We both listen. Nothing. I'm once again about to pull Madame away when the man breaks into a tuneless tra-la-la. This lasts for several seconds then is interrupted by a violent cough, a raw barking sound that causes Madame and me to jump away. The man bends over, makes a loud hawking noise and spits. "*Pardon Madame, Pardon Monsieur,*" he says wiping his mouth with the sleeve of his jacket. "In those years it was unthinkable that I would ever die."

"That's a very sick man," I say as we move on, "and crazy besides." I look back to be certain he's not following: the clarinetist hasn't budged, he stands in the pale light as silent and unmoving as a tombstone.

Madame does not speak for a moment then says, "His words had a certain logic, you know... Strange, but when I saw him approaching, I too thought of death... For a moment, as he spoke, I had the eerie feeling that he had plucked the thought from my own mind... *Voyons*, enough of this morbid chatter. Do you enjoy music, classical music?"

"Yes, but my knowledge is limited to Beethoven's Fifth and similar overplayed pieces."

"They offer chamber music concerts Tuesday evenings at the Salle Pleyel," Madame says. "I find it more intimate than a noisy symphony. Shall I see if I can find tickets? We can go this coming week." Her step quickens as we leave the garden and hasten toward the Place Rostand and the brightly lit cafes and the rushing traffic. The encounter with the sepulchral clarinetist seems to have given her a sense of urgency.

I hurry through the ancient streets of the Latin Quarter to meet Lea; the pavement is wet and the overcast afternoon seems a prelude to more rain or even snow. I have just picked up my monthly GI Bill check and keep touching the breast pocket of my shirt through my Army flight jacket to be certain the precious paper is still there. Actually, the check is more than paper, it's solid, substantial, like an oversized business card, pocked with little rectangular holes, a comforting reminder of efficient high-technology America.

Lea is already waiting for me at the bookstore Magnard on the Boulevard St. Germain, leafing through a book in the social science section. I once again admire how wonderfully slender she is; her clothes could, I suppose, be described as rags but I nevertheless find them attractive. A black purse is slung over her shoulder. "What are you reading?" I ask. She holds up the cover of a thick volume: *La Correspondance de Karl Marx et Friedrich Engels, 1846-1895*. "These guys must have had time to burn," Lea says. "They take simple things and babble about them for years."

As we leave I pause to look at the front page of *Figaro*. William Faulkner has just been awarded the Nobel prize in literature and his picture is beside the article. Grey hair and mustache, intelligent eyes, he could be a doctor, a psychiatrist maybe or a cancer surgeon who has given more bad news than good. You can't tell much by looking at a man's face. "Is that your ambition?" Lea says beside me. I'm not at all sure and change the subject. "I have a check to cash," I say. "Why don't we walk. It's not all that far."

We cross the Seine over the Pont St. Louis behind Notre Dame. The river is a muddy green-brown; the cathedral from the rear seems bizarre: it rises toward the lead sky like some outlandish Roman galley, its buttresses giant oars about to cleave the water. We reach the Rue Vieille du Temple. The streets are narrow, fractured, some blocked by reinforcing wooden beams that thrust against the cracked walls of the buildings; a *boucherie* displays the same Hebrew characters for kosher food that you see in Brookline. Men are gathered in groups of two or three; most wear worn dark blue or black coats, others suit jackets and knotted scarves, collars up. A fine cold mist starts to fall.

"I checked *Figaro* this morning," I say to Lea. "The rate is 387 to 393." I admire the pragmatic side of the French;

though the official exchange is 350 francs to the dollar, only wide-eyed tourists cash their dollars at that rate. To accommodate the rest of us, the papers publish the going black market exchange, referring to it as "the parallel market."

Lea approaches one group of three; I hang in the background. "I have a U.S. government check for two hundred and twenty-five dollars to cash."

The men eye Lea casually; all of them could use a shave. "365," says one of the men. He's not much older than I, skinny, stringy hair, tragic black eyes, a poet down on his luck.

Lea ignores him; he raises his shoulders, gives her a world-weary smile. "I don't have all day, messieurs," she says. "The paper says 400."

"Ah, the newspaper," says one of the others. The stubble of his beard is grey but his eyes are steady as a sniper's. "Why don't you ask the newspaper to change your money?" His breath smells of garlic.

Lea shrugs and moves away. "380," the sniper calls after her. She pays no attention to him and marches from group to group. "Messieurs," she says, "let us not be greedy. We're poor students. One more franc on the dollar means one more meal." She glances at me. I'm hunched against the cold, miserable, and want to get this over with. Lea jabs a finger toward me as though I'm an object on a fruit stand. "My friend is sick," she adds, "and needs medical attention." I cough obligingly and blow my nose in a grey drip-dried handkerchief. No one appears moved by this appeal, but I indeed begin to feel sick. I think of the clarinetist last night in the park. The exchange rate inches up; we're now at 388. "Let's take it," I say.

"Don't be ridiculous," Lea says. At that moment the sniper returns. "390," he says. "That's the last offer. No one will give you better. We have to live too you know."

"You have a deal at 391," Lea says.

The man sighs and casts his eyes skyward. "Pity the man who marries this woman."

"Yes or no?" Lea says.

He pulls a wad of franc notes as thick as a fist from his pocket, wets his thumb, and with the speed of a Monte Carlo cashier counts out the money. I do the multiplication on the side; the sniper never bothers. "By chance are you a Rothschild?" he asks Lea as he hands her the money; he smiles, his teeth splotched yellowish porcelain.

"Would I be here if I were?" she says as I endorse the check and give it to the sniper; Lea passes the bills to me and we're gone.

We wander back along the Rue de Rivoli and past the Hôtel de Ville. "That's got to be the biggest, fanciest city hall in the world," I say. Lea grunts in response. I can see something is on her mind. We approach the Tour St. Jacques, a grey gargoyled finger thrusting skyward through the mist. "Why do you think they built that?" I ask.

She glances up at the tower. "Maybe it was like an Inca temple," she says. "In case of plague, drought, whatever, they'd pitch virgins off the top. Placate the gods."

"Did it work?" I ask.

"Of course it worked. They just kept pitching virgins. Sooner or later the plague stopped, the rains started... Though they didn't have to use female virgins. Males would have been just as effective."

"It's easier to tell with females," I say, but I can see that Lea isn't listening.

The mist turns to icy rain. "Let's get out of the wet," Lea says, veering into a cafe. She orders a *café filtre* and a brioche then stares out at the rain and the street. I say something about my writing. She turns toward me but I can see her attention is focused elsewhere. "How's the book coming?" she says in a distracted way.

"That depends on the day you ask. Some days fair, most days, like today, lousy... What's really happened is that I've gone snow blind. Can't see the thing straight... How would you like to read a piece of it?, give me a critique?"

Lea has a way of listening to people, head cocked to the side, one eyebrow slightly elevated, as though she never quite believes, that appeals to me. This isn't happening now. "We've been through this," she says. "There's no point to it. All the scenes may be fine but the total book can still lay there dead on the paper. Until I see it whole, I just can't help you." It's the answer I expected but I thought I'd try anyway. She returns to a bemused contemplation of the rain and the hurrying pedestrians.

"Wouldn't it be great to be rich?" Lea finally says to the street. I can see what's been bothering her.

"What then?" I ask.

"I'd go south, to Cannes or Nice. Get away from the cold."

"What about school?"

"You're a constrained thinker, Franklin. Who needs school if you're rich?"

This isn't the first time Lea has wistfully spoken of her desire for wealth. My usual response is to make sympathetic noises. Now, her negotiation with the sniper fresh in my mind, I say, "Why are you screwing around with literature and philosophy? If money is what you want, why don't you go for an MBA, get into business?"

Lea shrugs and looks away. I wonder whether she will spend her entire life fighting this erroneous script that's been programmed into her head. When I met Lea's parents, her father worked as a translator for a textile machinery import/export company in Revere, and her mother taught French at a Berlitz on Beacon Street near the Boston Common. The old man, who had been an editor at a Paris left wing publishing house, realized early that being Jewish under Nazi rule was lethal, and escaped with his family to England in 1941, when Lea was fifteen, then immigrated to the U.S. after the war. He was sympathetic to socialism and Russia, and with great seriousness, between sips of camomile tea, expounded various screwball Utopia ideas to me, all in heavily-accented English punctuated with French noises. Once, when he mentioned France, he mumbled something about the virulent anti-semitism that had surfaced during the occupation and his face grew confused and child-like, as though he had been betrayed by his own mother, and for no apparent reason, and had heartbrokenly chosen never to see her again.

In one of my first conversations with M. Mervaud he quoted the results of a survey of teenagers conducted by Life magazine, asking them to list the Americans they admired most. Of the dozen names highest on the list, three stuck in his mind: Joe DiMaggio, Abraham Lincoln, and Doris Day. He asked me who the first and third names were and the role they had played in American history. I tried to explain but he seemed more baffled when I finished than when I began.

Lea's mother spent hours typing on an enormous Olympia the articles her husband wrote and sent off to literary reviews in France. Sometimes, as I waited for Lea, I contemplated M. Mervaud as he bent over the typed pages, his brow drawn together—scholarly, Talmudic, lost in an alien land—and I experienced a wave of pity, a desire to shield him. (The old man would occasionally seek a volume from a chipped glass-doored bookcase that leaned against one wall of the Mervaud living room. I was struck by the way he handled books—with respectful deliberate movements, as though a brusque motion would scramble the words inside and reduce the text to gibberish.) Lea gave me highly abbreviated translations of her father's polemics on the awful state of French letters. According to M. Mervaud,

French literary achievement had peaked with Victor Hugo. I had the impression that Mervaud once harbored a secret ambition to be a prodigious novelist, along the lines of his beloved Hugo, or Zola, or Balzac.

Words in the Mervaud household fluttered around me like exotic butterflies, lapidary comments on things literary or philosophical, alien to the jackhammer U.S. of A. that I knew. I felt tender and protective toward these outcast souls struggling to make ends meet in barbaric America. And this tenderness fastened itself on their daughter, in her intellectual interests and emotional maturity—not to mention her casualness with regard to sex—unlike any American girl I had ever met. When I think of myself in that year, viewed across the chasm of a lifetime, the image that comes to mind is that of a small boat, struggling on a tossed sea, bewildered and desperately searching for a harbor.

Lea's goal, unlike her father's, was to return to France. She told me she found America an intellectual wasteland and the Boston T in rush hour a modern equivalent of hell. Then she spoke lovingly of France. But I suspected that the France she spoke of was an idealized version of her girlhood experience and existed only in her imagination. She saved every cent possible: pennies earned tutoring French to students, correcting exam papers, doing translations. She finally accumulated enough money to buy a steerage ticket on the Ile de France and, on arriving in Paris, enrolled at the Sorbonne. She figured she had saved enough money to keep her going for a year on a starvation basis. But Lea had another reason for leaving the U.S. which I learned later.

As usual, I pick up the tab at the cafe. Lea ignores the bill when it appears and never mentions it when we leave or on the street afterward. She probably considers me flush after cashing my check, or maybe she figures I owe her a commission, but then she never pays or even offers to pay, so I don't know why I'm making excuses for her now. Her requirement for equality in all things except money is the most irritating thing about her.

We head back along the Rue de Rivoli. The sky brightens and you can make out the disk of the sun, thin, without heat. Tree trunks are wet and black in the watery light. Lea stops at a tobacco shop and buys a ticket for the *Loterie Nationale*. "Waste of money," I grumble.

"They hand out a billion francs a month in prizes," Lea says. "*Somebody* wins." She drops the ticket in her purse. I consider giving her a lecture on probability theory then decide it's a waste of time. At the Rue du Pont Neuf we head south toward the left bank. Lea pauses at the display window of the Samaritaine. "Let's look around inside," she says.

"What for?" I ask, still irritated over the bill at the cafe and knowing that she can't afford anything they sell. She couldn't possibly expect *me* to buy her something. Lea doesn't bother to answer but pushes open the door. She pays no attention to the perfume and makeup counters and finally stops at the hat, scarf and glove display. She spends virtually no time looking, nowhere near enough time for the salesgirl to approach and offer help, but with extraordinary rapidity stuffs a pale green silk scarf into her purse. Lea then dawdles at the counter, takes a hat and tries it on, studies herself in the counter mirror. For a minute I think she's going to shoot for a whole wardrobe. I notice the salesgirl approaching. "That's very chic," the girl says.

Lea smiles at her. "It's most attractive. Perhaps another time."

"Why did you steal the scarf?" I ask her on the street.

"Because I can't afford to buy it."

"God, Lea, you can say that about most everything in this world."

"Most everything wouldn't fit in my purse." She turns to me. "Think of it as part of my socialist upbringing." She says this with a smile and no trace whatsoever of guilt.

That evening I remember Lea's father explaining how simple and neat socialism is. "The state owns everything and everyone is a state employee." His eyes brightened as he said this, awed by the stunning simplicity of it and wishing to make a convert of me. "The state just calculates what goods are needed and produces them. Everyone contributes and is rewarded according to his abilities, but the disparity of income is not great. All of the citizens constitute the state and all are free and equal." I recall an edge of frustration to his voice as he explained this. It was all so easy, he must have thought, so straightforward. Why didn't Americans comprehend it? He never mentioned how the state figured out what goods were needed or for that matter how socialism handled stealing.

4

November 12.

I suspect each of us has an age, a fixed immutable internal age, at which he perceives himself for most of his life, regardless what the mirror says, regardless what the faces around him say. I am forever thirty-five; I can observe my husband of more than fifty years wander by (as though he were a soul that has been split in two and he searches forever for the part lost that would make him whole again), I regard the faces of Mme Parlanges and Mme de Hauteville, friends for almost as long as I have known poor lost Gustave, and know that I am no different from them. Yet in my heart I remain thirty-five.

November 13. I masturbated last night, a long slow caressing of my clitoris, and thought of the young man, of my François.

November 14. His French is improving; yesterday he referred to something as barbant and to a certain American

Senator as a casse-pied. *He could only have learned these terms from our conversations. The words startled me, as though I had unexpectedly beheld myself in a mirror. In a sense I am recreating François in my own language.*

Mme Colmar and I take the subway to the Salle Pleyel. Everyone bobs in unison as the train bobs (it seems to be traveling over a bumpy road), lurches in unison as the train lurches, and all stare into a void. "How sad everyone looks in the metro," Madame says. "How isolated. Here we are, packed like fish in a tin, yet no one acknowledges the existence of another. Sometimes I have the feeling that everyone on the train has died and is being transported to another world for judgement and each is considering how he will justify his life."

The train, almost full, stops at the Palais Royal station. While the door is closing, a black man tries to enter; his head is in but half his body still protrudes onto the platform, clamped by the door. His face is very black, blacker than American negroes, and his eyes are open wide, the whites stark white against the blackness of his skin as he struggles with the door. No one moves. I jump from my seat and with both hands pry the door open enough for him to slip inside. He glares at the door then smiles at me and while brushing himself off says in English, "Thanks a million. The fucking thing was about to cut me in half." He's American after all.

"That was a brave thing you did," Madame says and takes my arm. But I'm really not listening; instead I'm bedazzled by how wonderful the black guy sounded. I hadn't realized until that moment that I was homesick, that I missed my own fucking America.

"Look," Madame says, when we're seated in the Salle Pleyel, nodding toward an over-madeup woman in a black gown being led to her seat by a gnome-like man a head shorter than she and dressed in evening clothes. "That's the British Duchess de Milford, at least that's what she calls herself, and the man with her, who resembles Toulouse-Lautrec, is Guy du Plessis, the financier. They say he does not have a single virtue and is the most treacherous man in the world... Do you see the tall bent gentleman, the one with the patch over his eye? That's Georges Pellisard, a *député* to the National Assembly before the war who aspired to be prime minister. He had great energy and might well have achieved that august position except for a champagne cork. While opening a bottle of champagne for his mistress, the cork flew into his face. That incident cost him his eye, his mistress, his wife, and the premiership of France... Look to your left, the elderly monsieur being helped to his seat by two young women. He too was in politics before the war... tried to help everyone and was thrown out of office—a man undone by his finest quality." The man turns toward us: his face is ravaged as though he possesses some ruinous secret.

Madame comments on others, and though what she says is often not charitable, I can find no malice, only a hard-headed recognition of the way things are. I have no idea where she learns these things, locked in her Church of the Innocents. Anyway, I'm not listening too well. I'm back there thinking of America: Joe DiMaggio's 2000th major league hit, Teresa Brewer singing "Music! Music! Music!," and somebody who sounded like Teresa doing "If I Knew You Were Coming I'd've Baked a Cake," and wonderful redheaded Suzy Parker saying, "I thank God for high cheekbones every time I look in the mirror in the morning," and poor Joe Louis, who'd been the heavyweight champ since I was eleven, his bald spot gleaming discouragingly as he plodded around the ring, getting beat to shreds by Ezzard Charles.

The music is Schubert's Trout Quintet; Madame closes

her eyes at the opening chord of the strings and trill of the piano and settles back. I notice the diminutive financier meticulously picking his nose, the would-be prime minister adjusting his eye patch. During the *andante* I become aware of grazing touches against my hand: Madame is moving her fingertips in a slow caressing motion. The movement of her fingers follows the delicate exchanges between the piano and the strings, her touch weightless yet it seems to brush every nerve ending. I'm overcome by a sense of warmth, akin to the voluptuous relaxing I feel during our conversations, but now I also find that I'm sexually aroused. I glance at her and as though by some secret communication she turns toward me: her eyelids are slightly down, lips parted, and the wraith of a smile is around her mouth. I look away, take her hand in mine and try to concentrate on the music as we hold hands for the rest of the concert.

We take the metro to Odéon and cross the square to the Rue Danton. The air is cold and the wind blows in gusts; Madame turns up the collar of her coat and clings to my arm. I think of her thin body under her cloth coat and put my arm around her; I'm touched by the feel of her ribs against my fingers. We both seem to experience a sense of urgency and we hurry through the empty streets, arms fast around each other's waist. "I dreamt of peaches last night," she says in the dim hallway of her apartment as she takes off her coat. "Fat pink peaches... Does this mean anything?" She whispers this in the semi-darkness.

I can barely see her in the faint light. "Perhaps you wish it were spring or summer," I say. "Or maybe you were just hungry."

"Did you enjoy the concert?" she asks.

I hoist myself on the credenza, the wood smooth and cool against my hand. "It was very beautiful," I say, voice husky.

"Schubert was only thirty-one when he died," Madame

whispers. "Think of the terrible loss." She leans her head on my knee; we don't speak for a while. I can just see the outline of her. I feel that I'm about to fall into an abyss, want to get off the credenza, say good night and leave, but instead I caress her hair and the back of her neck. Madame touches my erection then unbuttons my fly and with great tenderness removes my penis and places her mouth around it. She is exquisitely delicate in her movements. At that moment the hall light—a furious torrent of illumination— is switched on. The figure in the bathrobe, his beard smeared with my chocolate, stands beside the switch. "Turn off the light!" Madame screams. The old man obeys. She returns as though nothing has happened and finishes the job.

There is a knock on my door. "My name is Berthe Colmar, Mme Colmar's daughter," the woman says. She is round-faced, heavy-hipped, fleshy, with small agate eyes, and does not resemble Madame at all; in fact, she reminds me of my French instructor at the Sorbonne. "My mother is out. I thought I would take a moment while waiting for her to meet the new boarder." She never apologizes for disturbing, but takes in the room with a critical glance then turns an appraising eye at me. "You are of her type," she says almost to herself, "though, I must admit, more hand-some than the others... Has she seduced you yet?"

I'm not sure of the verb. "Forgive my poor French," I say, "but what is it that you're asking? And who are these 'others?'"

Berthe Colmar scrutinizes my face, seems about to say something more but remains quiet. There are bluish cres-cents under her eyes. "What do you wish to tell me?" I say, filling the silence.

"My mother is in some ways a strange woman, with bizarre illusions of youth," she says, ignoring my questions.

"Do not be taken in by what she says."

"She has said nothing that struck me as bizarre."

"Just remember one thing," Berthe Colmar says slowly and carefully. "My mother has no money."

I can hear voices in the living room though my door is shut. "I will never agree to put Papa in a *maison de retraite*," Berthe Colmar says, her voice firm, solid, without emotion. I can't make out Madame's reply and open the door a crack; I justify this indiscretion as the legitimate curiosity of a budding novelist.

"You don't have to live with him, wash him, trim his beard," Madame says in a bitter voice that I barely recognize.

"He's Papa," the daughter says with finality.

"He's a faithful hound that trots along behind whoever feeds him," Mme Colmar says. "That's all he is."

My door opens and I jump away. It's old man Colmar. He looks around in his lost way, goes to the window and with surprising strength heaves it open, letting in a frigid November wind and dissipating in an instant what little heat was in the room. He pauses at my table on the way out and helps himself to a piece of chocolate. I shut the window.

"Papa is *our* responsibility," Berthe Colmar says. "Yours and mine. That's why I send you money. So he can be cared for by his own family and not by strangers."

"How touching," Madame says. "Well then, why don't you take him with you to Orléans? *You* care for him. Do this for a month. One little month. Comprehend what it means to be a prisoner in your own house. Then we shall see whether you still believe this lofty-minded philosophy."

"I have a business to run, *Maman*," Berthe says. "It's very difficult and takes all of my time. Where would we be without it?"

There is a silence. I imagine mother and daughter in the

45

shabby *salon* staring at each other across an abyss of disagreement while the old man wanders through the room nibbling my chocolate.

"I understand you met my daughter," Mme Colmar says. "What did she tell you? Did she say I was strange, to beware of me?"

"She was quite courteous," I reply guardedly. I'm uncomfortable with this conversation, though I'm not sure why.

"Berthe and I are very different, you know, not like mother and daughter at all. If I were her father I would question whether she was really mine. Alas, as her mother I can't very well do that."

"Perhaps if you spent more time—"

Madame cuts me short. "We have many differences that simply cannot be overcome. I live this way—" she motions toward the walls and her voice takes on the bitterness that I overheard in her conversation with Berthe "—because of her. My husband should be in a *maison de retraite*, but she refuses to pay for this, though the cost is not great and she has the money. So I'm condemned forever to carry the burden of him on my shoulders." She stares at me then drops her eyes and without energy says, as though it were something memorized, "My daughter is without gratitude."

"Ungrateful children have been with us for a long time," I observe, trying to comfort her. "Shakespeare's King Lear says 'How sharper than a serpent's tooth it is to have a thankless child.'" It comes out all screwed up in French.

"It's a terrible fate to be at the mercy of one's children," Madame goes on. "Berthe is not wicked, you understand. She helps in her own way. Her difficulty is that she cannot disentangle me from M. Colmar. She sees us yoked together like oxen, my fate inseparable from his. When I try to reason with her, to point out how ridiculous this is, she appears to listen but does not hear. But then she has never understood me. When she gazes at me, mouth open, I have the impression that she is staring at a rare and incomprehensible tropical bird. She cannot fathom the mystery of how it came about that I am her mother. And of course neither can I."

I find reasons to go out afternoons, attend more classes. The Sorbonne has been around for seven hundred years and the instructors sound as though they've been giving the same lecture all that time. I think of Mme Colmar as I shift position on the stone-hard seats: it's the brightness of her eyes and the power that seems to reside in her sturdy cheekbones that come to mind. I no longer think of her as old at all. But I stay away; once, sitting in class, before I dropped into a stupor, I had the uncomfortable feeling that in my relation with Madame I was the reluctant female being pursued. In the following days, when Madame poked her head in my room, I found I was abrupt with her, spoke in a more authoritative voice or answered in grunts as though too busy to be bothered. When I look at her now, it's her full mouth and slender body that I see; I know it's there for the taking but I can't bring myself to do it.

November 15. François has retreated like a frightened deer. How stupid of me to have been so aggressive! I must invent reasons to be together, let closeness work its magic, let him be the initiator.

November 16. Yesterday was François's birthday. He is twenty-five. What a splendid age! I bought him a pair of slippers, in handsome brown leather and lined with fleece. He walked around in his bare feet and risked catching a terrible grippe. When I presented him the gift I gravely turned my cheek to accept his chaste kiss of gratitude.

"How did you make out with Blithe Spirit?" Lea asks. We're at the Café St. Louis in the Place de la Sorbonne and I'm gazing across the square at the marble statue of Auguste Comte high on a pedestal. He appears translucent in the evening light as he stares dourly at the hurrying students. Lea repeats the question.

"He says none of his customers are interested," I lie. Actually, I haven't seen the bird man at all. I had planned to, procrastinated, then decided I just didn't want to be bothered. "By the way he said it, I think he just got cold feet and didn't propose the cortisone to anybody," I say, adding a little embellishment. "How are *you* doing?"

"I made two sales," Lea says, her voice businesslike but a light of triumph in her eyes.

"How are you going to handle it? I mean logistically."

"The pharmacists don't want to receive any packages in the mail. I'll hand deliver and they'll pay me right then. I called Vernon—collect. He agreed to send me the vials and I'll send him the money, less the commission, by postal money order."

"That's wonderful. Congratulations," I say. "But look, I'm pulling out of this deal. I wish you luck but in French at least, I can't persuade anybody of anything. Besides, this just isn't for me." Though I try not to, I'm afraid I give Lea the impression that I find the affair unsavory.

Lea shrugs. "It's up to you," she says. I have the feeling that she never did have high hopes for me as a cortisone salesman. She contemplates me across her cup of *café filtre*. "You don't look too good," she says.

In fact I've been headachy and chilled for two days and just want to lie down. "I think I've caught something," I say.

"Take aspirin with chicken soup," Lea advises.

A young woman enters the cafe and sits nearby; she carries a sack on which is embroidered, "What can I know?

What shall I do? What may I hope?"

"What do you make of that?" I say to Lea, nodding toward the sack.

"Those are Kant's questions," Lea says. After a while, after I had already forgotten about the sack, she adds, "All bullshit."

"Lea!" a voice calls from a nearby table; he's a fellow about my age, kinky red hair splayed in all directions, his complexion very fair, almost bloodless. The man with him, somewhat older, is tapping a Gauloise from a pack; the flame of his lighter delineates a flint face and glitters from what I take to be a diamond ring as he lights the cigarette. Lea introduces the kinky hair as Eric, a student in her philosophy class, and Eric introduces his companion as Hervé, obviously not a student. Lea offers only minimal encouragement but they join us at our table. I try to keep up with the French. The conversation shifts from the cold weather to an upcoming exam in ancient philosophy, Socrates to Aristotle, then to the war in Indochina. I say something negative.

"But you Americans have your own dirty little war in Asia," Eric says, having caught my accent.

"At least it's not a colonial war," I say. I'm being aggressive about this though I don't give a damn about Indochina—it's that I don't like the way Eric looks at Lea.

Eric switches the subject to the inflationary effect of the war on the French economy. "Many people profit hand-somely in a time of inflation," Hervé observes; he leans his hard face forward as he says this and speaks confidentially, as though imparting some privileged secret.

"How is that?" I ask.

"By investing in those things that increase in value during inflationary periods."

"Hervé buys and sells precious gems," Eric explains.

"In times of high inflation," Hervé says, still confidential, "people take money out of banks, where interest rates are now below inflation, and invest in precious articles—gems, art, gold—driving up their price."

Lea watches Hervé the way she observed Vernon. "I don't think you'll find two sous at this table to invest," she says.

Hervé lights another Gauloise, ring glittering. "We're only making conversation," he says. "But if you know anyone, your parents for example, who may be interested, here is my business card. These are fine investments." He removes two cards from his wallet and hands one to Lea and the other to me. It's an impressive looking thing, the print and a diamond reflecting a starburst off one facet embossed into the pasteboard. "I would give you a ten percent commission on any business you brought me."

I wonder whether Paris isn't full of hustlers, guys like Hervé and Vernon, pyramiding commissions; I suppose if you're interested you could spend your life peddling anything, from gems to drugs. But then, in one form or another, this must be going on everywhere, no doubt has been for millennia, worked its way long ago into the grain of the world.

When we leave I pitch Hervé's expensive card into the trash but Lea drops hers into her purse. For a moment I think she's going to add precious gems to her sales portfolio, alongside cortisone. "Are you really interested in that clown's proposition?" I ask.

"I wouldn't trust him with a hairpin," Lea says. "But why slam a door when you don't have to? You never know what opportunity may come along."

The conversation with Eric and Hervé has made my headache worse. "I think I'll take an aspirin," I say. I'm chilled again and not even up to going to Lea's room.

November 17. The date lies on the horizon, exactly five months off. I think of the intervening days as pages in a calendar to be grudgingly ripped, page by precious page. I must avoid the date becoming an obsession. It will grow with each passing week to the force of a whirlwind; knowing this I repeat to myself: remain calm, decide rationally. But to do this I must examine my antipathy toward Berthe, my own daughter. Where does it come from and why does it persist? One should love one's children, it's unnatural not to. I try to return to the beginning, when I was nineteen and Berthe was an unwanted weight that distorted my body... meaningless. Meaningless also when her greedy little mouth clamped itself on my breast. Berthe cannot be blamed for having been born. And what of Gustave? At least until Laurent came, he never tired of holding Berthe, played with her as young girls play with dolls, never scolded her; much later they sat together for hours as he taught her geometry, algebra, other mathematical nonsense. One would have thought the death of Laurent would bring us closer. Tragedy after all is supposed to bind a family together, but for us it did the opposite. Each of us grieved alone. Gustave retreated into his equations, back always curved, as though sorrow were a weight that rode forever upon his shoulders.

In womanhood Berthe developed a heavy rear and short fat legs, a reversion to the gross Germanic elements in Gustave's ancestors. Heaven knows I tried to share my own pleasures with her. But I don't think Berthe ever read a book or a poem she was not required to read or ever went to a concert unless I dragged her. I attempted to write to her, share my feelings with her. Her responses read like business letters. Has she had lovers? Does she have a lover now? All I really know of Berthe is that she cuts sheets of paper into patterns then cuts fabric and from this fashions gowns for the bourgeois women of Orléans. Does she envy these women? Does she imagine herself in luxurious gowns? Does she imagine anything?

What am I to Berthe? Certainly not a woman with needs of my own. I am but a caretaker for her father. A servant. Never once has she inquired how I spend my days. Nor can I recall a single instance when Berthe asked for my advice.

I search in my heart and conclude that what plagues me most is that I need Berthe, need her money. If she would pay for Gustave in a maison de retraite, *I would have nothing more to do with her, sell flowers on the street, anything, but be independent of her.*

There can be a communication between people, an understanding that exists without words being spoken, souls meeting. It is present in deep friendship, in love, but with Berthe... I never know what she is thinking; she answers my questions with distracted phrases, and information must be dragged from her like pearls from a clutching oyster.

The deepest hurt is that she has broken the chain of our ancestry and my most precious possession will stop with her.

There is still ample time to reason, to decide rationally. Growing old presumably one grows wiser, but I think whatever madness was buried in one's soul emerges and one becomes a bit crazy with age. I am not certain this is bad: a little folly in one's life is not improper.

I must search for wisdom in this matter.

5

"You don't appear

too well," Madame says. She places her hand on my forehead; it's surprisingly cool and comforting. "You have a fever. Best that you go to bed."

For four days Mme Colmar cares for me. She places an electric heater in my room against the cold. I mention to her that the effect on her electric bill will be a disaster. She replies that I'm *très gentil* to concern myself over her finances. She prepares a hot water bottle for me at night, and every four hours brings me a bitter tea-like concoction and a strange pill that resembles a small insect. When I'm apprehensive Madame tells me not to worry, it's a remedy against the *grippe* that has been used in France for hundreds of years, in fact by Louis XIV himself, and always works. She touches her lips to my forehead to check my temperature.

Madame feeds me soft-boiled eggs with bread cut into

sticks, soups, a baked apple with raisins in the cored out center, then sits and reads to me: excerpts from *Andromaque*, Racine's tragedy of the Trojan war and Hector's beautiful widow, the romantic poets—Lamartine, de Vigny, Alfred de Musset—and finally the letters of Mme de Sévigné. I often don't follow Racine: the French squeezed into twelve syllable rhymed couplets requires more concentration than I can muster, but his rhythms have a lulling effect and sometimes I doze off, then Madame lightly kisses my mouth and tiptoes out of the room. Her lips are cool and soft and I'm pleased that she's not concerned about catching my flu. When I'm awake and have taken my tea and medicine, she returns to her reading.

While Madame reads the plays and poetry with the feeling and diction of an actress, in the letters she reverts to her natural voice. I have the impression of listening to one side of an animated and witty conversation, in a direct style, easy to follow, all the more of a relief after the heavy Racine and the poetry. As she reads letters describing a walk in the country, the depth of Mme de Sévigné's love for her daughter, an event at the royal court, a burning at the stake, I feel that the words are not de Sévigné's at all, but belong to Mme Colmar, so deeply and naturally does she relate to them. On the evening of the fourth day, the feeling of tenderness, a relaxing tenderness that has been growing in me, takes on an urgent focus. I reach for her hand as she reads, all reluctance on my part gone. Madame stops reading and we gaze at each other. I find her face, illuminated by the light beside my bed, absolutely beautiful. I caress her hand. "Can you make love?" I ask.

"Yes I can," she answers, her face serious and lovely. I thought she blushed. I tug her toward me. "Wait," she says and disappears to return with a small white jar. She switches off the light; the only illumination in the room is the dim glow from the windows of the other apartments that surround the courtyard. She hurriedly steps out of her clothes and I strip off my pajamas. "You have a fever, *chéri*," she whispers against my mouth. "My beautiful feverish *Apollon*." My arms wrap around her and she around me, and as we press against each other I feel I have stumbled upon something, some elemental thing, that has always eluded me. We stay this way, clinging to each other, for a long while. In Madame's embrace I sense a desperate quality, as though she is clutching a raft on a stormy sea, then I become aware of a wetness against my cheek and realize that Madame is crying. "It is nothing," she says. "Only that it's so beautiful." And these words and the salt of her tears arouse me terribly and I kiss her face all over and she kisses me; as I prepare to enter her she gently holds me back and takes her jar and with great delicacy spreads a cream on my penis. And so Mme Colmar and I make love, I within her and her tongue alive and muscular in my mouth.

We don't speak for a long while, then Madame gazes toward the ceiling and once again complains about the ingratitude of her daughter. "I can understand," she says, "how with her character she never succeeded in attracting a husband."

I'm tired and drowsy in the aftermath, and also find that I have a headache. "Talk of your daughter only upsets you," I say and wonder whether I should take an aspirin.

"But you see," she says, "that's something else I have in common with Mme de Sévigné. She too had an ungrateful daughter, that she pined after, wrote to incessantly, and who dissipated de Sévigné's fortune and brought her only disaster."

Mme Colmar sighs and snuggles against me. "You know, there is a certain tie between Mme de Sévigné and my family. She corresponded with one of my ancestors, a certain Clémence Villandry. I don't know how often they wrote, but eight letters to her from Mme de Sévigné have remained in my family and are in my possession."

"They must be absolutely ancient," I comment absently.

"The letters have become something of a family heirloom. They have passed down the female line of my ancestors through eight generations."

"I'm surprised they have survived," I say, trying to stay awake.

"It's truly a miracle," Madame agrees. She doesn't sound sleepy at all. "The letters were written over the period 1662 to 1665, when de Sévigné was in her late thirties. They are perhaps not the finest of her letters but they possess much of her charm and immediacy all the same... Are you awake?"

"Yes, of course," I say, though I'm on the verge of dropping off.

"You know, I feel that to have them in my house connects me to the greatest epoch of France, through the long line of my family, and gives me a sense of belonging, of continuity. They're a great comfort. And I suppose a great treasure besides."

"Shouldn't you place them in a bank vault for safekeeping?" I ask. "The apartment may burn down or be robbed or some other catastrophe may occur."

"More catastrophe can befall a bank than this house. The letters have never been in a bank or anywhere other than in the hands of my various grandmothers in the three-hundred years of their existence. Why should they now?"

"I'm pleased for you," I say. "They seem to give you so much pleasure."

"Would you like to see them?" she asks.

I really don't care, but to please her I say, "Yes, certainly, but only if it's convenient for you."

"It will require a certain strength on your part to reach

them." She yawns and cuddles close. "We will do it another day, when you are well." Her breathing is even and I think she has fallen asleep until she says, "When I'm gone the letters will pass on to my daughter, and after that heaven only knows what will happen to them. She has no children and, given her age, never will."

Madame's breath is even and warm against my shoulder. I think in a dream-like way of the letters of Mme de Sévigné in the apartment. I too at this moment feel close to them, to the glorious past of France. Oddly, they seem to have burrowed into my mind and fastened themselves there: I imagine yellowed sheets of parchment with ragged edges, luminous as though they themselves were a source of light, covered with unreadable glyphs and possessing magical properties—like the diadems, crowns, scepters and staves of the pharaohs, they have the power to change one's life. I turn and take Mme Colmar's frail body in my arms and fall asleep.

November 23. Last night François and I made love for the first time. It was the most beautiful of moments and I tried to draw it out forever. Afterward I revealed to him the existence of the letters. I spoke of them in the most natural way, openly and comfortably, without hesitation. But reflecting on this now, the event is altogether extraordinary: never before have I disclosed the existence of the letters to a lover. Could something be occurring here? A leap of intuition? The guiding hand of Providence? I shall not be fanciful; simple explanations are best. There is something disarming about François that allows me to confide, to mindlessly babble whatever passes through my head. With him I feel no need to dissemble, to pose. Sadly, however, he showed only a remote and polite interest in the letters. But then how could I expect otherwise? Their value to me resides in the generations of my family that have possessed them and the importance of Mme de Sévigné to France. Poor François knows nothing of this.

When Madame considers me sufficiently recovered, she invites me to dinner and a movie. She takes me to *L'Homard du Roi*, a narrow restaurant on the Rue de la Huchette; waves are painted on the walls along with monstrous-looking lobsters, crabs, shrimp and other crustaceans that I can't identify. "*Ah, bonsoir, ma chère Mme Colmar*," the proprietor says to Madame when we enter and gives her a handshake of welcome. Mme Colmar introduces us and the proprietor nearly crushes my hand as he looks me over. I have the feeling that this scene has occurred before. He offers us a table near the window, away from the kitchen. The place smells of seaweed. Madame orders a mix of shell fish and a white wine called *Entre Deux Huitres*, served ice cold. "The ocean was the original source of life," she says, "and the ingredients needed to nourish life are to be found in those creatures that inhabit the sea." I'm finding that little theories undergird most everything she does.

The proprietor joins us at our table. His face resembles a topographic map of rough terrain. "You do not age, *ma chère*," he says to Madame. "You're more beautiful than ever." He turns to me. "You're in the company of an extraordinarily courageous woman, you know."

"Gilbert," Madame says, "you're not going to fill the young man's head with that nonsense about the *maquis*, are you?"

"Of course I am," Gilbert says. "Mme Colmar was a courier for the resistance during the war. She crossed and criss-crossed Paris delivering messages, often after curfew. Sometimes she lugged weapons and ammunition. All at supreme risk to herself."

"It was no great thing," Madame says. She seems genuinely embarrassed by the subject. "Many did far more."

"She was apprehended by the Germans."

"I played the muddled old lady," Madame says with a shrug. "It was not a demanding role. That was the night I learned the German word *verrückt*." She shrugs again and gestures with her hands. "Anyway, you can only die once."

"Yes, but it lasts for such a long time," Gilbert says and gives her a wintry smile.

Madame slips me money when it's time to pay.

The film Madame takes me to is Jean Cocteau's *Orphée*, starring Jean Marais. Mme Colmar's mouth is slightly open and she leans forward in her seat whenever Marais is on the screen. When we leave the theater, Madame gestures toward a cafe across the street. "Shall we have something before we face the cold walk home?" The cafe is half full, too warm; we place our coats on the backrest of an empty chair, Madame's purse on the seat; a couple about my age occupy the adjacent table. Madame orders a Calvados for both of us. "I first saw Marais in the chorus of Cocteau's version of *Oedipus Rex*," Madame says, "and thought him a young god. I followed him from then on: with Madeleine Sologne in *The Eternal Return,* where Cocteau insisted that Marais and Sologne go to the same hairdresser so they could have the identical hair color, with Yvonne de Bray in *Les Parents Terrible*, and in *The Eagle with Two Heads*."

While Madame speaks, eyes shining with enthusiasm for Jean Marais and *Orphée*, I notice her purse on the chair, as though a mysterious act of telekinesis were taking place, move ever so slowly along the seat toward the adjacent table. "Did you notice how brilliantly and with what economy Cocteau used the supernatural?" she says. "He even endowed it with a set of laws. The cinema is very different from the stage, isn't it? It creates a hypnosis of light, dehumanizes the actors. They become supernatural beings, gods. I once saw Jean Gabin signing autographs and while doing this he scratched his private parts. I was astonished and commented on this to Gustave." She sighs. "My husband did not find it at all remarkable."

I can see the shoulder strap of the purse stretched taut and disappearing under the table where the couple is chatting and paying no attention to the object heading in their direction. I reach over, grab the purse before it vanishes, and yank the strap from whatever is holding it. Madame is startled as I hand her the purse; I gesture with my head toward the couple who, as though they were living in a parallel and unrelated universe, continue to yak. Their faces suddenly appear too bright, bleached and without dimension, like an overexposed photograph.

"There is some robbery that has a certain dignity about it," Madame says when we are on the street. "A thief with a gun in the Bank of France is at least forthright in his actions and intentions. But someone who sneaks through windows and steals while his victims sleep is truly despicable."

I try for a philosophical note and quote M. Mervaud quoting Machiavelli, "He who wins by deception deserves no less credit than he who wins by force."

"Do you really believe that?" Madame asks turning toward me.

"No," I reply.

Mme Colmar now uses the intimate *tu* when we converse. I still employ the respectful *vous* but she never suggests that I change. She also calls me by my first name but Frenchifies it. I have been called Frank as long as I can remember but Madame finds the k sound too harsh and insists on calling me François. "But your name starts with a k sound," I said when she started this.

"That's one of the reasons I hesitated before marrying my husband," she replied.

We pass two workmen, visored with glass, one is welding a tramway rail; the arc of his acetylene torch is like a miniature sun throwing off yellow and green sparks; the men are eerily lit, the intense light reflecting off their masks. Madame pauses to watch. The air smells of ozone. "It's as though they are repairing a soul fractured by some terrible accident," she says. "Like the soul of the foolish young man who tried to steal my purse. One does not have to go to the cinema to view the supernatural."

In the corridor of her apartment, Madame hands me a small box wrapped in blue paper. "A gift," she says. It's a fountain pen, the name François engraved on the barrel. "This pen," she says with great seriousness after I give her a kiss of thanks, "will turn you into a Stendhal, or a Zola at the very least." She holds me at arms length, wrinkles her brow and stares at me. "You know, *chéri*, you should grow a mustache. That would make you more handsome yet."

We go to my room. The little white jar now sits on the nightstand beside my bed. Sometimes the door opens and M. Colmar wanders in; at first he gives me a start and is quite inhibiting, but then, taking my cue from Madame, I learn to ignore his ghostly presence. (I have checked the luminous dial of my watch: M. Colmar does indeed have a pattern, like the postman he always wanders by at about the same hour, though whether he will throw open the window or not seems to be a matter of chance.) Afterward I hold Madame close and feel strangely protective of her frail bird-like body, still capable of so much passion.

Madame never again mentions the Sévigné letters. Perhaps it was the fever, but that whole conversation has become unreal to me. Several times as we snuggle together I'm on the verge of mentioning the letters but never do. I'm surprised to find something avid in me when the letters force themselves on my mind, a morbid curiosity that's unsettling, and I push the thought away. But it always returns: I explain it as a desire to see this paper that

Madame treasures so, to participate more fully in her life, to establish whether the conversation really happened. The letters seemed to provide her with solidity, certain knowledge that she is but one of an endless chain that will endure forever. It must be splendid, I think, to have that kind of assurance. It is indeed the sort of thing I would grasp for and hallucinate in a time of fever. Though I find this explanation unsatisfying I do not search for another, hoping that thoughts of the letters, like the recurring dream of slow and agonized running from approaching disaster that I experienced as an adolescent, will disappear and not trouble me further.

6

The early December
cold is much worse than November. Madame wears two sweaters, adds a sweater under M. Colmar's bathrobe; I wear my flight jacket while at my desk and buy more chocolate. I try to work but often find myself staring at the ancient pen and ink sketch on the wall in front of my desk. It's entitled "Plead Not Guilty" and depicts a sly attorney whispering to a disreputable-looking client. I have become a student of that picture and can, I think, draw it from memory.

Lea rarely goes to school now but spends her days cruising the pharmacies. You have to admire her tenacity, whether laboring over Proust or selling cortisone. We see less of each other. She has moved to a new apartment, on the Rue Jacob, further away. The place has a kitchenette with a stove, a small refrigerator and even its own bathroom. An oil painting of Montmartre and Sacre Coeur hangs above an attractive wooden desk. "The pharmacists are leery, the customers are leery, and Vernon's price is too high," Lea says. She's seated on a stuffed chair, wearing a new dress and high heels that set off her slender ankles. She looks splendid but, oddly, less desirable. "Besides, one pharmacist told me he's been approached by another salesman offering cortisone, and at a lower price."

I can see that Lea has become a businesswoman, concerned with marketing, competition, price. "You don't appear to be doing badly," I say, gesturing at the apartment around us. I'm awed by her ability to make something of nothing.

"I've got to call Michael and discuss this."

"Who's Michael?"

"Vernon. Michael C. Vernon. Remember? I want to be certain that *he* hasn't recruited the salesman. He's got to be tidy as to who's assigned what territory."

I feel a need to get out of her apartment; the place seems to change our relationship, makes me feel diminished. But everything about her now makes me feel shrunken, including the way her head tilts upward when she looks at me, as though I'm located somewhere beneath her.

"I have to make a delivery to a guy on the Rue La Fayette," Lea says. "Why don't you come along, then we'll have an early dinner." She drops a small package, wrapped in blue paper, in her briefcase and we take the metro to Chaussée d'Antin. When we reach the pharmacy Lea glances at me—the appraising look. "That's an awfully mousey looking mustache," she says.

"It's just starting to grow in," I say, defensive though I'm not sure why. "I'm trying for a Faulkneresque look."

She checks me out again. "Why don't you wait outside. I won't be long." She turns and, looking professional as hell, enters the store. I feel as though I've just auditioned for a part and been rejected. I turn up the collar of my old flight jacket, thrust my hands in my pockets, shift from one foot to the other, and contemplate the piece of the Opéra visible down the street: a figure is perched on the corner of the building and silhouetted against the fading sky, wings extended. I have the impression that the poor thing is in the clutch of frozen stone and just can't break loose. A young woman passerby slows to observe her reflection in the pharmacy window—she appears moved, touched by the view of her own face.

I think of my writing and Lea. In Boston, when Lea critiqued my stories, her marginal notes were brutal but right. She scribbled things like "nothing is happening—this reads like oatmeal;" or "all these people sound alike;" or "who wants what?" or scrawl an accusing black circle around a phrase, which meant cliché. I came to depend on her critical judgement and when she finally wrote "this is good!" it was the exclamation point that gave me the greatest satisfaction. I sent the story off to the New Yorker and after a time, a long time, they returned the manuscript together with a lemon-colored rejection slip. Lea waggled a dismissive finger. "Most writers can paper the walls of a room with their rejection slips," she said. "If you can't handle rejection, you should stay in engineering." My writing became bound to Lea; when I left for Paris I told everyone it was to take a crack at writing, but even as I said it I found myself thinking of Lea.

"Let's get out of the cold," I say when Lea emerges from the pharmacy.

"Don't knock the cold weather," Lea says. "It aggra-vates arthritis and that ups cortisone sales." Her eyes narrow as she says this; I attribute it to raw greed rather than the low temperature. We walk along the Boulevard Haussmann, the Galeries Lafayette to our right. Lea slows to peer into the display windows; we pass one entrance, a second, then a third; at the fourth entrance Lea veers into the store. I sigh and follow. She sprays a counter sample of *Miss Dior* on her hand and dabs it beneath her ears, then brings her head close to mine. "What do you think of this?" she asks.

I find the odor musky, whore-like. "It's very sexy," I say. The small jar disappears into her purse. "You never wear perfume," I say. Lea's shoplifting, I have concluded, is independent of her financial condition. It no longer surprises or even bothers me, rather it's a mild nuisance, like a facial tic or a stutter that one overlooks after a while.

"It might be useful one day," she says. "You never can tell."

She strolls over to the clothing counter and tries on a dark green beret, a beautiful color that sets off the green of her eyes, walks away, looks around further, then leaves the store, the beret still on her head. It occurs to me that she never did any of this in the U.S., at least not in my presence. Maybe here, freed from parental constraint or obligation, she feels she can do whatever she pleases. She wasn't keen on any of America following her to Paris. When I broached the idea of taking my last GI Bill year at the Sorbonne and concentrating on a novel, she wasn't encouraging, just skeptical as to whether I had the guts to do that. I think that's what convinced me to go. She had already left when I packed my B-4 bag and bought the cheapest possible one-way ticket on the *America* for Le Havre. The one hundred and twenty-dollar price emptied my bank account.

"I'm starved," I say when we're on the street.

Since, despite the improvement in Lea's fortunes, I always wind up paying, Lea is rather easygoing as to where we eat. But I've developed a system. I avoid the restaurants on the main avenues and check the side streets, looking for small establishments where the menu is handwritten in purple ink, checking a single item on the menu: porkchops. These will cost anywhere from 500 to a 1000 francs, or about $1.25 to $2.50, on the boulevards, but I've found them as low as 300 francs and perfectly acceptable on the sidestreets.

"There's a little place on the Rue de Mogador called *Chez Pouquet,* she says. "Why don't we go there?" The name, she tells me, is that of the young woman who was Proust's model for Albertine, one of the few characters in Proust's immense book that Lea claims had any appeal for her. The menu at *Pouquet* is indeed in purple ink but the porkchops are 450 francs. I'm too cold and hungry to object. I decide to go with porkchops and lentils, the cheapest dish on the menu. Lea orders fish. "I never eat anything I can pet," Lea once told me. I learned much later that this was a favorite line of George Bernard Shaw's. I'm astonished at *Miss Dior*'s staying power; I can smell the musky scent across the table despite the restaurant odors. I can't say that I dislike it.

For some reason—probably my homesickness returning—I steer the conversation to Boston and the university. The name of the restaurant must have triggered thoughts of her failure there because Lea says, "I think what happened is that I just got tired of Proust. You can't believe how dull it is trying to follow his transcontinental sentences and all that introspection. He's just a snob, really, and a spoiled adolescent snob at that."

"What happened to your thesis?"

"You'd be amazed at how many theses have been written on poor sickly Proust. But there was one that I thought truly good, written by a woman at BU the year before me. Her view was that Albertine and Odette were the real heroes of the novel. I used some of the ideas from that one. Anyway, my professor, Runge was his name—always smoked a pipe and had a lousy accent in French, something of a clown really—didn't agree with the premise and rejected the thesis. He did surprise me in one way. I always thought him absent-minded, but he put a copy of the essay where I'd gotten the idea in the envelope with my thesis when he gave me the failing grade." I can see Lea's face tightening at her recollection of the treacherous Runge whose memory had returned in time to sink her thesis.

"Maybe he thought you'd used too much of the other woman's work," I say, avoiding the word "plagiarized."

"Don't lecture me on what is and what isn't proper source material," Lea says in disgust. I can see this is a delicate subject and talking about it has put her in a bitchy mood. It occurs to me that Lea's relation to her thesis is not very different from her relation to the beret that now sits on her head.

I pay at the restaurant and as usual Lea behaves as though no bill even exists. I consider commenting on this but, under the influence of *Miss Dior*, decide against confrontation. We take the metro to St. Germain des Prés. The train is crowded and we hang onto a pole, the metal cold and greasy in my hand. The train lurches then picks up speed and squeals around a curve; on the straights there is a steady roar through an open window and everyone sways and appears catatonic. Contrary to Lea's wistful recollection of the metro when we were in the U.S., I don't find this superior to the Boston T (which at least has the advantage that some of its routes are above ground) but decide to wait for another time to make this observation. Lea doesn't utter a word throughout the trip. She stares at a sign that says you have to give up your seat to pregnant women, disabled war veterans, and aged persons. Someone has written *"merde"* on the lower right in a handsome script as though signing a painting. An olive-skinned couple, probably Arab, the woman very pregnant, enters the train at Châtelet. Everyone looks through them as though they were invisible. The woman is still standing when we get off four stops later; I think of the sign and make some comment to Lea about racism in France but she just grunts, apparently elsewhere. We go to her room; I'm not happy about this but there's nowhere else to go. The place now reminds me of a hotel, makes me think of a whorehouse. "I don't much care for this place," I blurt out.

"Why not?" Lea says. I now notice there are dirty dishes piled in the sink. She must have followed my glance because she says, "Do you think the place is a mess?" There's an aggressive edge to her voice. She tosses her new beret in the closet.

"It could use a little straightening," I say, trying to stay neutral.

"Well, next time we'll go to *your* room. You can introduce me to your cultured old landlady."

"I'd be glad to invite you," I say. "It's just that Mme Colmar is adamant about no female visitors. She put the warning in her listing at the school housing office. Even repeated it when I first showed up."

"Hogwash," Lea says, then sits at her desk under the Montmartre painting and arranges some papers, her profile sharp and hard as granite. *Miss Dior* is long gone.

"What is it that you want, Lea?" I ask.

"I don't know," she says and looks down; when she raises her head toward me, her face is broken up and she's crying, a slow pained rolling of tears. I'm astonished and, I must say, not displeased at this show of weakness. I go to comfort her but she pushes me away. "I never go to school, I'm unhappy with men... I'm making money but feel like I'm just drifting around... miserable most of the time..." That plural 'men' bothers me.

"What does it take to fix all that?"

"Money," she says, her face hardening. "Not this penny ante shit but lots of it. That's what it takes. Lots of money."

"Well, you're on your way."

"No I'm not," she says, her expression morose. "How

long do you think this is going to last? Sooner or later some French company will get approval to sell cortisone and they'll put me out of business."

December 11. Why do I keep this journal? To slow time, to live each moment of this last year of my life twice, to savor each instant again as I write of it, to clarify my thoughts. What shall become of this journal? Inconceivable that Berthe find it or, what amounts to the same thing, that it fall into the hands of a stranger. The day before I die I shall destroy it. Pity I don't have a fireplace—I imagine these pages, one by one, days of my life, being consumed by flame.

Like a traveler after a long sea voyage seeing the outline of a landfall, I begin to see the shadow of my own death.

December 15. Passion opens one, exposes the vulnerable center of needs and fears. I know I can open myself to François, there is no wickedness in him. But my life has been so darkened by separation and death that if I care for someone the possibility of loss immediately wraps itself like a shroud around that person. I try to love obliquely as it were, to care less, to fool destiny. I desperately want François to remain with me, to comfort me, until the end. It is after all not far off. I feel the clotted grip of anxiety. But then anxiety has always been a part of me, shadowed my life. Perhaps that is why I have always tried to hold the moment, draw it out, for fear that another like it may never return. Perhaps this anxiety, this fear of loss, is what fuels passion, has forever made me desperate.

Mornings, Madame spends an hour at her desk in the *salon* and writes in a green-covered ledger-like notebook. She seems refreshed after she has done this. She sometimes disappears afternoons, usually Tuesdays and Thursdays, to visit friends. There are only two that she ever mentions,

Mme Parlanges and Mme de Hauteville. She adores them both and describes their idiosyncrasies in loving detail. I can always tell which she has visited by her subsequent conversation. Mme Parlanges sees World War III and atomic bombs raining on Paris in every international incident, the price of food rising so they will all become *clochardes* scavenging the markets for leavings, the Bank of France failing, the church in conflict and the Pope about to resign. As far as I can determine, these predictions are based on the scantiest of data, a casual comment in the market-place, a back page article in the newspaper. "To appreciate Mme Parlanges," Mme Colmar says, "you must under-stand that she sees the world as an extraordinarily compli-cated place, filled with unlikely connections, more complex than any of us can imagine. For her, all reported events are oversimplified and fail to elucidate the underside of things. Mme Parlanges believes in the conspiracy theory of life, that everywhere forces in government, business, the church, are conspiring against ordinary people like us. The newspa-pers are of course not permitted to speak of this, or else are themselves part of the conspiracy." Madame recounts this to me with amusement, and once told me, as proof that Mme Parlanges has a brighter side, that the woman loves *les histoires paillardes*, dirty stories, and has a great stock of them. She picks them up in the marketplace and appar-ently remembers them all. The one I recall Madame repeat-ing to me concerned a man who was complimented by a woman on his broad shoulders. "All men from the Midi have broad shoulders," he said. Later in the evening she complimented him on his powerful thighs. "All men from the Midi have powerful thighs," he said. And later yet she complimented him on the dimension of his masculine organ to which she received the usual reply about the men from the Midi. When they were well into lovemaking the man paused and said to the woman, "Tell me, what part of the Midi are you from?"

Aside from seeing disaster around every corner, Mme Parlanges's favorite topics are murders and executions, taking precedence over government corruption and war. I have no idea where she obtains the information, but she retails it to Mme Colmar, recounting the grisly events with enormous gusto, greatly pleasing Madame. I visualize her at a window in some protected sanctum, edging aside the curtain to cast a suspicious eye on the world.

Mme de Hauteville claims she was born in the wrong century, the preferred one being the seventeenth, and from what I gather many of her beliefs are of that epoch. She and Madame read aloud to each other, usually poems and plays. Mme de Hauteville prefers Molière and she and Madame read *Le Bourgeois Gentilhomme* or *L'Ecole des Femmes* or *Tartuffe*, dividing the roles between them. In their readings, familiar pieces do not easily stale for them. They can read *L'Ecole des Femmes* twice in a month and if anything enjoy it more the second time. Or they dip into obscure pieces, like *Monsieur de Pourceaugnac*, that are never performed. "If Mme de Hauteville has a defect," Madame tells me, "it's a too great preoccupation with her health. She runs from one quack to another at the most casual suggestion. She has tried coffee enemas, drinking sea water three times a day, sitting under electric arcs, eating the organs of lizards, and heaven knows what else. It's a tribute to her constitution that she survives these things." I gather that Mme de Hauteville is always asking Mme Colmar for advice and since, as Madame herself would no doubt observe, no one gratifies more than a friend hungry for advice, Mme Colmar parcels it out in large dollops and is always ready to give more.

Both of Madame's friends are widows and speak of their deceased husbands as saints. They both have children and though Mme Parlanges rarely mentions hers, Mme de

Hauteville's requests for advice often concern her oldest son, though I suspect he has never asked for advice nor heeded it when given.

I gather that these women rarely do any errands or services for each other, but exchange confidences and anxieties. Madame overlooks Mme Parlanges's baleful view of the world and Mme de Hauteville's hypochondria, loves them both, and elevates them to divine status. I conclude that to be befriended by Mme Colmar is to be automatically exalted and I suspect that if she ever mentions me to her friends, I too am raised to an Olympian level.

December 26. We exchanged gifts. I gave François a wool scarf. The weather has been extraordinarily cold and this will help him ward off chills, fevers, etc. He presented me with a book, Camus's The Plague, *attractively wrapped in red paper, and even bought a gift for poor Gustave, a package of madeleines. Much as I detest cooking, I prepared a Christmas dinner for us, a cabbage soup and a rôti of veal (I used the vegetables from the soup to garnish the meat). I found the veal tough but François ate with great appetite as did Gustave. The bottle of Chambertin was excellent. I overcame my antipathy and invited Berthe, but to my relief she declined saying that she was behind in her work on gowns for the New Year's festivities.*

January 1. I would have liked to bring in the new year with François but he disappeared yesterday evening and has not yet returned. I find bitterness and jealousy creeping into my heart over this. How foolish of me! It is reasonable that he should occasionally seek the company of fellow students, men and women of his own age. I may as well envy youth as be jealous of his time away from me. Yet as I sit here now and write, I find that I am really listening for his footsteps in the hallway. It reminds me of those mo-

ments in my childhood when I would hide in the hope that someone would search for me.

7

I try to work.

Madame claims this is the coldest winter in a hundred years and has returned the electric heater to my room. I have it standing on the chair adjacent to my desk. I eat oranges, touch the rind to the heating elements and enjoy the sizzle and sweet odor, a bit like Cointreau, that rises from the singed peel. In my novel it is almost Christmas, the marriage of the hero has ended in disaster. He wanders the streets of Boston on a drizzly evening, zigzagging past the shoppers, debating whether to buy his estranged wife a gift, a silver pin in the shape of a soaring bird that she had once admired. There is an animated display of an abandoned child trudging in the snow in a window of Jordan Marsh. The hero stops behind a crowd of onlookers to watch. Everybody around him smells of rain. A ridiculous song is playing: "poor little fellow, poor little fellow was he." The hero can relate, but he's certain that at least for the little guy in the window a good samaritan will soon show up, the kid's luck will change. It's the way to bet given that it's a Christmas display. The hero doesn't wait for the outcome but leaves. He decides to buy the silver pin and send it to his wife with a clever note. I can't figure out what the note should say.

Madame pops into my room. I can tell that she has just returned from a session with her tarot reader: she's in an excellent mood and crackling with energy. If one believes, it must be a compelling experience, like psychotherapy, to have one's own life at the absolute center of attention, objectified in the images on the cards. "Why don't we go out this evening," she says. "Let's not sit here like birds in a cage." She places her hands on her hips, surveys my face and frowns. "First let me trim your mustache," she says. "You're beginning to look like one of those sinister Prussian officers." She darts off and returns with her glasses and a pair of scissors, then, squinting and admonishing me to be still, her face extraordinarily serious and beautiful, she trims my mustache, hair by hair. That evening she drags me off to the Palais de Chaillot where the Opéra-Comique is doing *Tosca*.

The air outside is heavy and less cold than it has been in weeks. On the metro Madame gives me a sketch of the major characters—the jealous Tosca, her star-crossed artist lover, and the lecherous head of the Roman police—and a summary of the plot. The whole thing sounds preposterous. It's the first opera I have ever attended; we're seated high in the third balcony; the place is the size of Fenway Park, crowded, hot as hell, and smells like a locker room. I don't know what's going on but Madame—who squeezes my hand when the big arias are on the way and joins in the applause when they're over—sits on the edge of her chair through the whole event. At the end of the third act, when Tosca blessedly leaps off the parapet to her death, Madame turns to me, her eyes entreating and blurred with tears, as though she had expected me to save poor Tosca, and says, "That was the most beautiful opera I have ever seen."

On the way out, Madame comments on the decor: "Great staircases are the vice of mediocre architects," she says, shaking her head as she damns most of the architects of France. A crowd is stopped at the exit. "My God! Look!" Madame exclaims. No one else appears awestruck, most just look pissed. White flakes are swirling in the lights; in the Trocodero Gardens, on either side of the exit, a delicate scrim of white covers the upper branches of the trees; sounds are muffled. I feel that I'm inside one of those miniature globes that has just been jiggled. I think of my novel. "Let's enjoy it and walk home," Madame says, "before it's all soiled by automobiles and people."

"It's a long way," I say. "Besides, we don't have an umbrella."

Madame waves her hand in a grand gesture. "It's only three or four kilometers, François. A little snow won't hurt you."

She holds my arm as we cross the Pont d'Iéna. The Eiffel Tower before us is a shadow on the whirl of flakes, the lattice limbs curving upward and disappearing into the dark. We follow the quai along the river; hunks of ice float in the water and reflect the lights of the right bank like huge phosphorescent eyes; the lights themselves are surrounded by haloes of white. It's late and no one else is walking; we leave fresh footprints, Madame's straight as an Indian's, mine splayed outward in a herringbone pattern; the headlights of an oncoming car trap the flakes like clouds of moths then the vehicle rolls past, oddly quiet, leaving black tread marks in the snow. Madame raises her head skyward and opens her mouth. "I'm catching the snowflakes," she says. "As a child I was fearful that the white falling from the sky would alter—instead of snow it would become chalk or salt—something choking and horrible." She stops and looks at me. "*Chéri*, you have snow in your hair and on your eyelashes." She brushes my hair. "Close your eyes." She gently brushes my eyelashes and kisses me. It's no ordinary kiss.

"Do you want to take the metro home?" I ask.

"No, let's keep walking. This is too beautiful to miss."

We pass the Pont des Invalides and kiss again. I notice a horseshoe-shaped cavity in the parapet along the quai and draw her into it. We make love leaning against the stone, her head thrown back, snow falling on her upturned face, mouth open. As I come I hear a muffled crash from the bridge and through the swarm of snowflakes see a pair of headlights askew, facing upriver—apparently one car has skidded into another.

"That was a splendid climax," Madame says as she adjusts her clothes. I wonder whether she's referring to the collision on the bridge.

I cash a GI Bill check and buy Madame a bouquet of red roses. Damn the expense. "Oh, *chéri*, they are magnificent!" she says as she places them in a vase on the coffee table in the *salon*. She puts an arm around my waist and we both stare at the flowers. Then I notice she's crying. "It's nothing," she says wiping her eyes. "I'm just a foolish old woman... Roses in this season. How wonderfully extravagant of you, François." We hold each other's waist and stare at the magical flowers.

Despite the cold and the slippery sidewalks, when the weather is at all decent, Madame invites me for a stroll. She takes my arm and as we walk points out small details that catch her eye, usually stone ornaments on a building—the winged head of a woman, coiled dragons around a window, lion heads protecting a doorway, a child listening at a seashell. One evening we wander along the narrow passage of the Rue de la Parcheminerie, the buildings angled to each other like blocks set down by children; gas lamps high on the walls throw golden ellipses of light on the cracked stone facing, the irregular cobblestones. We turn on the Rue St. Séverin—the street goes through sudden darting changes of direction as though created by a water bug—and reach the Rue Privas. A couple on bicycles pass us, filling the street.

"All of Paris was once this way," Madame says, "a splendid hodge-podge of buildings, full of medieval charm and the enchantment of another age. It was the infamous Baron Haussmann together with Napoleon III, with their passion for the rectilinear, that remade Paris into the orderly array of dull thoroughfares you see now. A triumph of the straight line. Geometric savagery. After walking for an hour on those avenues one would give anything for a street that turns." She sighs. "Thank heaven they never reached our little corner."

One late afternoon we walk along the quais and cross the river to the Place de la Concorde. Chunks of ice like marble slabs float down the Seine and in the distance form a solid blue-white sheet across the river. The Tuileries look like an abandoned graveyard. In the Place de la Concorde we both stare through the twilight at the vast square, the obelisk, the flow of automobiles, buses, bicycles. "Things are terribly hurried now," Madame says. "People rush so. They seem so purposeful. It must be the effect of the motorcar. Another day we'll stroll on the Ile St. Louis. One still sees medieval idling there, gossip passing from shop to shop, people a little slower, a bit careless, more easily diverted." While Madame is musing, I gaze at the equestrian statue of Mercury nearby; he holds a winged staff with entwined snakes and gives off a bronze glow; I think of Vernon and cortisone and Lea. The great fountains look naked and abandoned without the water running. A forest of lights suddenly goes on and seems to emphasize the statues, all of women wearing crowns and enthroned on stone chairs.

"They make me think of my great uncle Albéric, my grandmother's brother," Madame says toward the statues. "He was a stonecutter, grey dust permanently lodged under his fingernails and embedded in the lines of his hands. When I was a child he sometimes took me to his *atelier* and, in the powdery half-light, I studied the headstones and statues he carved. The statues troubled me. Then all statues began to trouble me. I complained to my grandmother that statues often stared at me, and they were neither sympathetic nor kind. *Grandmaman* told me that statues imprisoned the souls of sinners. They were sentenced to watch us and read our minds and only when they found sinners like themselves to replace them in the statues would they be set free... Since then I always hurry past statues and avoid their eyes."

As we leave Madame says further, "I used to think of this square as the hub of Paris. Now I think it's the hub of France." I gaze at the obelisk in the middle: it seems a great spike that fastens the square and everything around it—the avenues and monuments and buildings of the city, the countryside around it, indeed all of France—mountains and rivers, farms and cities—to the center of the earth. To me the square looks like the hub of the world.

We return to the left bank across the Pont de la Concorde and follow the Seine eastward. Lights from the right bank reflect off the river in long shimmering bands interrupted by the glint of ice. A cold wind is blowing across the water; we both lean forward; Madame holds my arm and we don't speak for a while. She seems in a reverie. We approach the Pont Royal: the side of the Louvre rises from the opposite bank like a fanciful ocean liner adrift on icy black water. "Mme de Sévigné was an indefatigable walker," Madame says à propos of nothing. "Another time we'll walk to the Place des Vosges and I'll show you the house where she was born." Madame then falls back into her reverie and doesn't bother to look up or comment as we pass the Gare d'Orsay. We turn away from the Seine on the Rue du Bac—a floral pattern in stone, delicate in the light of the street lamps, decorates a wall.

"You see the man approaching?" Madame says, straightening now that we're out of the wind. "The one with a newspaper under his arm? He's kindhearted, considerate to his wife, his children, his colleagues." I let this go by. A woman hurriedly crosses the street and passes us without a glance. "I would guess she's unfaithful," Madame comments, "and unhappy with her life."

"On what basis do you make these judgements?" I ask.

"Years of observing people," she says, then smiles and gives me her impish look. "But really it's only fancy. You can never know another simply by regarding his face. It's just a game I play. I like to imagine the character and the life of strangers—on the street, the metro, anywhere. Sometimes to amuse myself I imagine them as other than human—as a species of animal, as flightless birds, as insects..."

"Suppose we met now for the first time," I say. "What character and life would you ascribe to me?"

"Alas, *chéri*, it is too late for that," she says, her expression genuinely sad as though she has disappointed me. "Now that I know you I cannot imagine you other than you are—a loyal and noble-minded man, no more capable of deceit than changing the color of your eyes. As for your life, only the tarot can give you an answer."

A young woman passes by, coat drawn tight around her body, high heels clicking on the pavement. Madame must have followed my glance. "What is it that you find attractive about her?" she asks.

It had never occurred to me to analyze these things. "It's difficult to say," I reply. "...her legs, buttocks... the way she moves..." I'm uncomfortable with the subject. What I don't tell Madame is that the woman reminded me of Irene, and the things that made Irene so attractive—a mixture of innocence and lust, frivolity and seriousness—were beyond the physical and too elusive to describe.

"If you tire of an old lady and occasionally desire a young woman, I can arrange that," she says.

"But I already see a young woman," I blurt out, not sure why I say this.

Madame lets go of my arm and is silent for a while. Her hands are now thrust in her pockets and her posture is more erect, more rigid than usual. "Describe her to me," she says. Something irritatingly possessive has entered her tone and her attitude. I decide not to reply. "Why don't you answer?" Mme Colmar persists.

"What is it that you want to know?" I say. "What difference could it possibly make?"

"Is it a serious affair?" she asks, voice abrupt, impersonal.

"No. Not at all."

We walk on in silence. I notice a sliver of moon wedged in the branches of a tree. Madame stares at the night air in front of her. "It's of no importance at all," I repeat, and take her arm. We walk this way for a moment longer then she stops and asks, "Are you sure?" There is a pleading expression on her face that I find heartbreaking. "Absolutely certain," I say and kiss her and hold her close to me; we stay this way for a long while, then we continue to walk, arms around each other's waist, the rest of the way to the Rue Danton.

January 19. Yesterday afternoon I accompanied Mme de Hauteville to the flea market, this time the Marché Brion in Clignancourt. As always, de Hauteville had no particular item in mind but wandered through the maze of stalls looking for some treasure of another era. She loves to haggle. Last year the purchase of an eighteenth century sideboard took most of an afternoon. Yesterday she was obsessed with a nineteenth century Gallé vase. I am amazed at her patience, her ability to insist on a ridiculous price then only slowly and reluctantly increase it, her choice of moment to walk away (but not too far). The bargaining for the vase lasted three hours. I nearly froze to death. After the ordeal, Mme de Hauteville appeared refreshed and left with an air of triumph, as though she had just negotiated the purchase of the Suez canal; the poor merchant seemed exhausted, ready to close his stall. I must say, I find most of the bric-a-brac at the Marché Brion just old trash, somebody's discarded junk, and only went at the insistence of Mme de Hauteville and the pleasure of seeing a master bargainer at work, one who must surely have Arab blood in her veins. But something far more important than a display of de Hauteville's haggling skills took place at the Marché yesterday.

Perhaps I was overtired by the long outing in the cold, but as François lay beside me last night, breathing evenly, sleeping the untroubled sleep of the innocent, I remained awake. As I stared into the darkness, hands folded across my chest, an idea came to me, rather it appeared as a scene, as though on a stage, that played itself out before me. In a strange way I believe it was brought on by the Marché Brion and the old vase. The idea was so enormous that I considered it an aberration of the night, one of those outrageous thoughts that occurs in the dark when one cannot sleep and whose foolishness is revealed by the first light of day. But as I sit here and write, the idea remains, still waiting to be judged. In this affair I know that intuition alone will not do, rather clearheadedness and good sense are needed.

The idea must have been forming as I watched de

Hauteville bargain because while this was happening it crossed my mind that I would like her, or better yet Mme Parlanges, to meet François. Why would I think this? I have never arranged this before. Yet the thought is sound. When one is always alone with a person it is difficult to form an objective opinion of his worth. Alone, I may read too much into the young man, create of him a fiction, a product of my own imagination. Seeing him with others, and therefore in a sense through the eyes of others, a more dispassionate appraisal will be possible. Yes, I will arrange a meeting— it will be revealing to witness François being interrogated by Mme Parlanges, and will help me judge the worth of the idea.

"André Gide died," Mme Colmar says in the best of humors. She shows me a photograph in the newspaper of Gide lying in state on an iron bed in his apartment on the Rue Vaneau, wearing what looks like a heavy sweater and a nightcap. "Even in death the poor man suffers from the cold," Madame comments. I scan the accompanying article; they have published the epitaph he wrote for himself—it reads like a résumé, as though the guy were applying for a job. "Why does death always lead to exaggeration?" Madame says. "François Mauriac, who should know better, calls Gide's literary work the most significant of our time." She waves her hand and dismisses the Nobel prize winner as though she were shooing away a fly. At that moment M. Colmar wanders by. "Gide was a geometrist, as he was," she nods toward her husband. "Too much head and not enough heart." The old man pulls aside the curtain and thin sunlight filters through the streaked window and onto the faded rug. Madame, who apparently guesses what is about to happen, yells, "*Non!*" but too late. The old man has hoisted the window wide open to the icy February cold; she hops off the couch to undo the damage. It's tough to imagine M. Colmar having too much head.

Lea has disappeared. Vanished. She's never in her apartment and never at school. Maybe she's been arrested. I imagine her in the Bastille, chained to a wall, unspeakable acts being committed on her body. I briefly consider asking the police, then, in a more sober moment, decide to wait. My feeling is that sooner or later she'll surface. For a lunatic instant I'm tempted to ask Madame for the name of her tarot reader. I wonder whether subconsciously I'm not integrating into Madame's crackbrained world, taking on her medieval beliefs. But where the hell *is* Lea? When I last saw her she had just turned down my luncheon invitation. Taking in the freezing streets with a wave and obviously in a splendid mood, she declaimed, "St. Agnes Eve—Ah, bitter chill it was!" and recounted the legend that a virgin who fasted all that day would behold her true love in a dream. "Isn't it a bit late for that?" I grumbled, not sure what was going on but unhappy about it all the same. "You never know," she said, too coyly, and with a small goodbye gesture, disappeared.

8

Madame takes me

to the Salle Gaveau to hear Ravel's string quartet. "It's a wonderfully profound work, you know. Better than any chamber work Brahms ever composed and exceeded only by Beethoven and Schubert." She says this in a friendly didactic way, always surprised at how little I know.

"Tell me about education in America," she says one afternoon between sips of Cointreau.

"Mine was a technical education," I say. "It had little to do with the humanities."

"What a shame. But you are very young and have much time before you to learn. Let us read to each other a little each day. In this way you will come to appreciate the grandeur of French literature."

In reality, Madame does all the reading. She stresses poetry, ignores chronology as she jumps from the works of Baudelaire to La Fontaine, and tries to explain the charm of each piece. She claims Apollinaire is of mixed worth but at his best is sublime and Verlaine a case of arrested development, a perpetual adolescent. So, in the soft intimate light of the lamp beside the faded blue sofa, wearing granny reading glasses, Mme Colmar recites French poetry to me. Sometimes I lose concentration, daydream, then the words slip past me like soap bubbles, rainbows diffused on their surface. Madame's eyes when she looks up try to convey the splendor of what she is reading and at one point she broke into tears. "It is too beautiful," she said. Madame has taken charge of my education in the humanities. I tell myself that I should be working on my book, but I seem to have lost my way. I go back, review the earlier chapters, check my outline (which now seems simple-minded), then try to plunge forward, write anything, desperate to put something on paper. But this often peters into lassitude, my head filled with mush, and I find myself doodling or staring at the sly attorney and his gullible client. I'm relieved to get away. And so I neglect my writing and never bother going to the Sorbonne as I become the student of Mme Colmar.

Madame decides on an outing to the Louvre. She holds my arm as we walk along the Quai des Grands Augustins. There's no question of taking the bus or metro. The transportation workers are on strike for higher pay. I sympathize with them—the price of porkchops, my bellwether, has risen by a quarter in the five months that I've been in the city. The strike started in Paris and has now spread throughout France. *Figaro* had a picture of the Gare St. Lazare, normally jammed with commuters, now uninhabited, the empty train shed and converging tracks resembling an architect's drawing. The weather has broken in a violent upswing in temperature and simultaneously a fog has settled over the city; traffic crawls, sounds muted, figures appear suddenly out of the mist; across the river the spire of St. Chapelle is blurred, ghost-like, as it appears then disappears into the fog. Though we are far from the ocean, the mist hints of salt and carries an intimation of the sea. Madame's voice is muffled as she speaks through the scarf wrapped around her nose and mouth; she claims the damp air is bad for her lungs. "Isn't this strange?" she says. "One imagines limbo this way, everything indistinct, disjointed, frightened souls peering into mist, trying to discern their future." She hugs my arm. "Too much cinema," she says. We pass the Pont Neuf where the statue of Henry IV astride his horse is just visible: he appears a mad phantom galloping through the fog.

When we enter the museum, Madame stops before the Winged Victory of Samothrace. "Some things are more beautiful when imperfect," she says. "It's difficult to imagine this sculpture in its original state, where no imagination is needed to define it, being superior to this. It's the viewer's inventiveness that makes it a masterpiece." I have to admit to the Victory's extraordinary grace. Mounted as she is on a stone pedestal that resembles the prow of a ship, leaning into the wind, she is both sensual and exalted. Mme Colmar is right: I cannot imagine her other than she is.

We move through the galleries. Madame likes Gericault, thinks his *Head of a White Horse* a masterpiece ("he has captured the essence of 'horse'"), considers his *Raft of the Medusa* one of the great paintings of the world, finds Rembrandt's later self-portraits filled with pathos.

She takes me to a small portrait, its width no greater than the span of a stretched hand. "This is my favorite painting in the entire museum," she says. I check the descriptive plaque, it's Vermeer's *The Lace Maker*, then I notice the date of the canvas: 1665. At that moment, with the precision of a cash register ringing the amount of sale into its little window, the dates of Mme Colmar's Sévigné letters, 1662 to 1665, materialize in my mind. "How intimate it is!" Madame says. "Everything is precise, down to the lace bobbins in the young woman's hands, yet somehow it's filled with poetry. Renoir declared it the most beautiful painting in the world." But I'm not listening to Madame's effusions over *The Lace Maker*. Instead, her words, whispered in the dark as she lay beside me, reappear, wraith-like, as though they had once been living things. As we move away from Vermeer, I know, know with certainty, that while Madame's revelation of the letters may have been distorted by my fever, there was nothing hallucinatory about it. How stupid of me ever to have thought so! The letters exist somewhere in her apartment. Madame comments on Poussin's *Orpheus and Eurydice,* Fragonard's *The White Bull in the Stable* (it reminds her of a summer in the country with a great Aunt when she was a girl), but I remain riveted on the letters, only now my curiosity focuses on where the letters may be hidden. *"It will require a certain strength on your part to reach them..."* Are they under some weight, concealed beneath a floorboard like Poe's telltale heart, or sealed within an impossibly thick container like those buried time capsules?

I notice there are no other visitors. Middle of the week, lousy weather, transportation strike—only the Mme Colmars of this world would trek to a museum. Madame pauses before another Fragonard, *Women Bathing*. "Notice how insubstantial and bubbly the painting is," she says. "The whole canvas looks as though it were created of foam." I'm on the verge of blurting out, right there, in front of all those pink nipples and rosy rear ends splashing in the foam, "I want to see your Sévigné letters. This afternoon. Now," though I don't understand this sudden madness, this obsession with the letters. Instead I look away. My eye is caught by the portrait of a woman on the opposite wall: she is seated straight-backed, on blue brocade, grey hair pulled back, her refined bony face alive with intelligence, and a self-possessed impish smile, identical to the smile Madame often gives me, animates her eyes and mouth. I check the plaque: it's the portrait of a certain Mme de Sorquainville by a fellow named Perronneau. I imagine her as one of Mme Colmar's ancestors, a third generation possessor of the Sévigné letters. I turn to look for Madame and find her beside me; for a moment we gaze at each other: her slender face seems itself to be a work of art, fitting in perfectly with the portraits and landscapes and still lifes around us. "What is it François?" she asks.

"It's a great pity that I cannot paint," I say, "because I would like nothing better than to do your portrait."

She kisses my lips and I experience an upsurge of desire as though it were some terrible emergency. For an insane moment I wonder whether the place has an Egyptian wing, like the Boston Museum of Fine Arts, a remote corner without guards. I could fuck Madame behind one of those broad-shouldered blank-faced statues, or hidden by a winged lion or a sphinx or a stone coffin, anything. "Let us go quickly to where we can be alone," I say. We hurry from the museum and with relief I thrust the letters from my mind.

At the Carrefour de l'Odéon a woman with an incredibly florid complexion is selling the first flowers of the season off a cart. Perhaps it was the visit to the museum, but the lavender mist that persists over the city now seems mixed with art and the view along the Boulevard St. Germain resembles an impressionist painting. I buy Madame a bouquet of Parma violets (they're only 400 francs); her gesture of surprise and the fuss she makes arranging the flowers on the table in the *salon* are a delight to me. "Napoleon was a great lover of violets," Madame says as she adjusts the stems. "They were the only flowers Josephine wore at their wedding and when she died he insisted that only violets be planted on her grave. Napoleon always carried a few of those violets in a locket, which was found around his neck at his death." We place our arms around each other's waist and gaze at the delicate purple flowers and smell their sweet fragrance. "How beautiful!" Madame exclaims as though she were contemplating a painting she admires. I think of poor Napoleon, wandering around St. Helena, dead violet petals hanging from his neck.

The following evening we return to the Salle Pleyel where somebody named Walter Rummel performs Beethoven's Moonlight and Pathétique sonatas. Madame prefers the *adagio* sections to the stormy bow-wow passages. After the recital, she suggests we go to Les Halles for onion soup, but when we exit the metro she says, "My desire for onion soup has passed. What I would adore is some ice cream. Come, you will taste the best ice cream in Paris." She wears her impish smile as she says this and pulls me by the arm. Her manner alerts me that this is no corner soda fountain she's taking me to. "What exactly is this place?" I ask, leery over this sudden enthusiasm for ice cream in winter.

"It's an establishment recommended by Mme de Hauteville," she says while hurrying along. "She guarantees I'll find it amusing."

A woman appears under a streetlamp on the Rue St. Denis, in high heels and wrapped in a fur coat, hands in her pockets and leaning against a wall, eerie in the mist. She might be a statue except that her head moves a trifle and her eyelids flicker as we pass. Only the whores in Paris seem to wear fur coats, but I suppose it's necessary in their profession, otherwise they'd freeze to death out there on the streets. Or maybe only the ugly ones would freeze. Madame pays no more attention to the girl than to the streetlamp.

A sign in blue neon script at eye level reads *Le Chien*

Bleu, and a doorman in uniform directs us downstairs. We enter a low-ceilinged room, dimly lit, where the patrons are arranged in a horseshoe pattern around a central stage. After we are seated I look around: most of the patrons are older women, well dressed, in groups of two or three. There are few men. The stage is suddenly lit and a young man in a business suit steps out and places a chair in the center. Madame motions to the waiter; he shakes his head, points to the young man, says something. "Nothing is served while the spectacle is in progress," Madame whispers, "but he can take our order." She asks for a Martell and I a crème de menthe and we both order vanilla ice cream.

The man on the stage removes his jacket and places it on the chair. He then, in the most leisurely manner, removes his tie, then his shoes and socks and starts to unbutton his shirt. There is slow jazz music in the background. I've gotten the picture. "Did Mme de Hauteville mention that this place featured striptease?" I ask.

"I'm sure you will find the ice cream exquisite," she whispers leaning close, then darts her tongue into my ear. I pull away, irritated by her gesture, and sense the onset of depression. The man takes off his shirt to reveal a muscular torso. Mme Colmar, her head now resting on her hand, watches, a half-smile on her face.

The stripper is now in boxer shorts; Madame does not take her eyes off him. I try to say in French, "We're about to find out whether there's a divinity that shapes our ends," then give up. In a graceful gesture, he strips off his shorts and is revealed in a slender athletic supporter covered with silver sequins that glitter in the lights. The supporter is held in the back by a thin line of fabric that disappears in the crease of his muscular buttocks. He strikes various athletic poses and rotates slowly, blows a kiss at one woman, wiggles his tongue at another. Then in a final motion he sheds the athletic supporter by undoing a snap in the back.

His dong is purple-colored in the lights, uncircumcised, and, I must say, of formidable proportions. There's a subdued "oooh," like a sudden wind through branches, that traverses the audience. He rotates slowly for all to get a good look then leaves the stage to applause.

I manage to say in French, "Well, we got to see his finer points." Madame squeezes my hand.

Our drinks and ice cream arrive; Madame raves about the richness and texture of the *glace* and I respond with positive noises, but frankly it's not nearly as good as Breyer's in the much-maligned U.S. of A. Suddenly there is a musical fanfare and a spotlight is shone on two elderly women at a nearby table: one is absolutely ancient, her face in the brilliant light striated and sagging like melted wax, and her spine curved as though bent by the weight of her head. The waiter serves them drinks and strawberry ice cream in silver bowls. The ancient woman's ice cream is different from the others: it is in the form of an erect penis. The waiter sets it down with a flourish, the curve of the penis bent toward her. The waiter steps aside, the spotlight stays lit, the room quiet, all eyes on the thousand-year-old woman. She contemplates the pink ice cream, then grasps the bowl with a liver-spotted hand, adjusts its position, bends down and places the head of the penis in her mouth. She receives a nice round of applause, louder than the stripper. The spotlight goes out and the woman raises her head: there is pink fluid on her lower lip. She throws her head back and laughs, a loud jarring cackle. Everyone laughs with her. "I suppose they chose her for the special ice cream because she was the oldest woman in the room," I whisper to Madame, then realize I'm talking to her bad ear. "That was very amusing," Madame says. She seems refreshed by it all. I feel sad as hell.

Mme Colmar holds my arm as we hurry toward the metro; there's barely enough time to catch the last train. I'm depressed and sense that it has something to do with the stripper and the old woman and me and Madame. An oily night mist films the paving stones and Madame, humming *Auprès de ma Blonde*, takes a false step and slips, causing me to slip with her and we're both on the ground. She looks at me and her eyebrows raise and she starts to laugh, a rich full-throated laugh, but underneath, like a distant echo, I hear the cackle of the ancient woman. Though I laugh with Madame my depression does not lift. Two gendarmes on bicycles stop and tell us we're being too noisy. Madame sobers up and we brush our clothes as she says to the cops, "Wisdom and love are not made for each other." The cops look us over without cracking a smile, salute and cycle off. At the metro station four derelicts lie huddled against a wall like victims of a firing squad. One is snoring. It's more depressing yet.

March 5. I continue to think of the letters but with no resolution and increasing despair. Sometimes I see them in the hands of Berthe, lost amidst sewing machines, meters of fabric, clothes dummies, other times I see them in a museum, the Carnavalet or some such place, on display like Egyptian artifacts or Gobelin tapestries, the dead remains of a remote epoch, glanced at by bored strangers. If only there were a way for the letters to be reborn, start life afresh.

I have procrastinated over the idea that occurred to me after the visit to the Marché Brion with Mme de Hauteville. I think I'm afraid of it, of where it leads. But the thought nags at me and time grows short. A solution is necessary. Yesterday evening I finally summoned the courage to say to François, "I would like you to meet my friend Mme Parlanges. I'm sure you will find her interesting." François gallantly said he would consider it a privilege to meet my friend. I shall arrange this in the next few days.

9

Mme Colmar and

I are walking along the Boulevard St. Germain; we've just passed the bronze statue of Diderot (the feathered end of a quill protrudes from his extended hand as he makes a point), his face streaked with pigeon shit, when I notice Lea coming toward us. Even with Madame on my arm I experience a twang of pleasure at seeing her again. Lea raises her hand and waves at me in the funny way beautiful women wave. I introduce her to Mme Colmar. To my surprise, Madame says, "Why don't we three take something at a cafe. We're close to the Brasserie Lipp, a charming relic of another era." I have misgivings about this: it's too European for me. Then there's no way to know what Madame will read into our glances or how she will interpret what Lea says. Lea, though, thinks it's a fine idea and readily agrees.

Lea is wearing a light green topcoat that I have never

seen and is splendidly tanned. "Where've you been?" I whisper as Madame negotiates a table with the maître d'.

"Cannes," she says.

Despite myself I ask, "Alone?"

"No, with Michael."

Madame orders tea and an assortment of cheeses and cakes. We're across the street from the Café Flore and Les Deux Magots where existential babble about Why Are We Here? and What Is The Purpose Of Our Lives? goes on in continuous session. I have to agree with Lea: listening to it is like watching traffic—always different yet always the same.

"What do you do, Mademoiselle?" Mme Colmar asks.

"I'm a student," Lea says. To me at least, Lea doesn't look like a student at all. She has removed her coat and is wearing a nubby linen dress, in light green as well; she's also now wearing perfume and it's no longer *Miss Dior*. "I'm studying philosophy and French literature at the Sorbonne," she adds.

"She wrote a thesis on Proust," I chip in.

"That's a large undertaking," Madame says. "What was your conclusion?"

Lea shakes her head in a short rapid side-to-side motion. "I thought the hero a self-indulgent snob. He spends his time drowning in reverie, or paralyzed by endless analysis. I found much of the book inconceivably boring."

"It's a coincidence that you're interested in Proust," Madame says, "because I met him."

Lea stares at Mme Colmar. "You *met* Proust?" It was as though Madame said she had met God, or at least St. Peter.

"It was in 1921 or 1922, toward the end of his life. We were with acquaintances at a nightspot called *Le Boeuf sur le Toit* and were joined by a man who appeared to have just emerged from a nightmare. I remember that his hair hung in damp bangs and he had a thick mustache; his eyes were close together, heavy-lidded, and accented by dark crescents. He moved slowly, as though under water, and had a strangely barreled chest. The man never shed his overcoat though the room was warm—he seemed imprisoned in his clothes—and said something about his health in a soft wheezing voice. Everyone by then had drunk a great deal and I don't think anyone listened to him. The man was introduced by his friend at the table as the writer Marcel Proust, the man who had won the Prix Goncourt one or two years before, and someone offered him champagne. It's difficult to remember a casual encounter that took place thirty years ago, and more difficult yet to convey a man. There is after all an essential mystery to a human face that you cannot dispel simply by describing it. But I do recall that at one point Proust stared at me: his gaze was terribly fatigued yet as it fixed itself on me, it seemed to enter, diagnose, and judge without emotion. I felt totally revealed though I had not said a word."

"Have you read his book?" I ask.

"After that encounter I read the *Recherche*, or at least much of it. I would agree with Mademoiselle that there are dull stretches. But the novel after all is about growing up and growing old, about our inability to truly possess another human being or to know someone we love. Difficult subjects and perhaps at bottom somewhat boring. But he did succeed in conveying another world, much of which throbs with the very beat of life. That's no small thing."

"I think it unreasonable for one to spend so much time chewing on the past." Lea says. "I mean, didn't you find something morbid about his wallowing around forever in the lost paradise of childhood?"

Madame shrugs. "To some extent, yes. But then, Mademoiselle, what paradise is there to regret other than one you have lost? Perhaps you would do better returning to Proust when you are older."

I can see boredom settling into Lea's face.

"I have recommended certain readings in French to François," Mme Colmar says, nodding her head toward me, "but these are the classic authors. Perhaps you can suggest more modern writers. For example, I have been most impressed with Camus, much less so with the fiction of Sartre."

"I think François had best concentrate on completing his own book before embarking on an extensive reading program." I detect irony in Lea's voice as she calls me François. The Proust story caused me to reflect on Mme Colmar's age: it occurs to me that she is old enough to be our grandmother.

"I notice that we are once again about to have a change in government," Madame says. "Of course governments come and go, what concerns me far more is the rise in the cost of food, twenty percent in the past year."

"The Socialists will bring all that under control," Lea says. "That's the future for all of us." She says this with great certainty; I can hear the voice of M. Mervaud. "Look at the Labor Party victories in England, the growth of socialism here and in Italy. The model of Sweden, Russia and the Eastern European countries—"

"What a horrible fate," Madame says. "to have a faceless state, an army of *fonctionnaires*, control our lives."

"We had all best get used to it," Lea says. "But the control of inflation is difficult and will no doubt take years to achieve. In the meanwhile, the French franc may well take on the value of the German mark during the Weimar Republic." It's always a surprise to me to hear Lea speak French; she somehow becomes more sophisticated, persuasive.

"How do you protect yourself against this?" Madame asks. She seems too concerned and I have the impression that she does not truly care but only wishes to learn more about Lea.

"By investing your money in those articles that will always retain their value," Lea says, leaning forward. "For example, while money may become worthless, diamonds never will. Paintings by the masters are another example— a Renoir or a Monet can only increase in value... I have access to precious gems at ridiculously low prices because of distressed situations resulting from the war. If you are interested in art, I'm sure I can procure for you original masters at bargain prices." I stare at Lea's newly tanned face as she says these things, astonished at the audacity of her proposals and the confidence with which she makes them. I can hear the confidential voice of Hervé and catch the glitter of his diamond ring as he lights a Gauloise at our table at the Café St. Louis in the Place de la Sorbonne, across the square from the marble bust of Auguste Comte.

Mme Colmar's eyes narrow as Lea makes her proposition. "These things sound most interesting," she says. "I will certainly consider them. It's good of you to counsel and offer to assist one who is ignorant in these matters."

Madame pays for our snacks. At home she asks me, "Are any of the investments your friend proposed worthwhile?"

"Only you can judge," I answer.

"But what is your opinion?"

Madame stares at me: I sense an important moment. "I would not give Mademoiselle Mervaud one sou," I say.

"Thank you, François," she says. "That was a brave reply and I respect you for it. For a moment I thought you would allow your friend to swindle an old woman."

Lea and I are sitting at the Select; I don't know why she picked the place—it's touristy and filled with Americans still expecting F. Scott Fitzgerald to walk through the door. I'm about to ask when a tall blond man in a suit and tie, a splendid tan and a huge smile, approaches our table. "Hi

Lea," he says and kisses her mouth. "Sorry I'm late."

"You remember Michael," she says to me.

"Vernon," he says while sticking out his hand. "Michael Vernon." I put down my beer. He's still smiling as we shake hands; he seems to have an extraordinary quantity of teeth.

"Michael is on a quick trip to Paris to attend a conference on leukemia," Lea says. "He's pressed for time so I asked him to join us."

Vernon orders a rum St. James. "That's what F. Scott Fitzgerald used to drink in this place," he says. "It seems like the proper thing to imbibe here. Homage to the great man and all that." Vernon's horn-like voice has not changed. He now sports aviator style glasses; they give him a dashing look.

"I think you're confusing Fitzgerald with Hemingway," I say.

"I thought Fitzgerald was the drunk," Vernon says.

"Scotch kind of drunk," I say. "More patrician than rum."

I can tell by the way Lea is staring at me that she thinks I'm being obnoxious. In fact Vernon and Lea are both staring at me as though they expect me to say something more. They remind me of movie stars, tanned in winter, filling their space with well-being, expensive clothes, sophistication. They seem to be expanding before me. I feel shrunken, suddenly aware that I need a shave and my clothes are taking on a *clochard* appearance.

Vernon lays his hand on Lea's, a large capable hand sprouted with golden hairs. "This lady is the finest pharmaceutical salesman in the world," he says to me, aviator glasses scintillating. "She's doing the arthritis sufferers here an enormous service."

"One day she'll be canonized for her work," I say. "I'm sure arthritics can use a patron saint."

Vernon sips his rum and makes a face. "I can't imagine

what Fitzgerald saw in this stuff."

"Another reason why he drank scotch," I say.

Lea has removed her hand and is now watching me over her cup of *café filtre*; it's the appraising look. "You've lost weight," she says. "Your face is thinner."

"It's the artistic life," I say. "Sick emaciated guys write better."

Vernon adjusts his glass, saucer, napkin, and the ashtray so they form a rectangle, gazes at me benignly, then looks out at the traffic. He suddenly jumps to his feet. "By God!" he exclaims. "There's Noel Coward! I wonder what he's doing here." I look out to see a man running across the street in a fruity way toward a cab. "Probably looking for Scott Fitzgerald," I say. Lea gives me a dirty look.

Vernon sits down. "How are the subagent appointments coming?" he asks Lea, voice suddenly professional.

I gather that Lea has recruited other salesmen, all students, to visit pharmacies in areas she hasn't covered. She mentions Montrouge, Ivry-sur-Seine, Courbevoie, and other suburbs. Apparently she splits the commission with the subagents. I finish my beer, swipe at a fly, stare out at the traffic on the Boulevard Montparnasse and the comings and goings at La Coupole across the street, and sigh, a long deep sigh, the death of hope. I can't top Vernon's Noel Coward sighting. The two of them babble on about other territories, sales to hospitals, selling directly to doctors, and other bright marketing ideas. Vernon even has the gall to suggest advertising. I hope they both wind up in jail. I look down and notice a dog, a black terrier, lying under an adjacent table. We stare at each other; the pooch doesn't look too happy either.

Finally Vernon glances at his watch, calls for the check, kisses Lea and whispers something that causes her to laugh; he then gives me an affectionate pat as though I'm a household pet, a left-over smile on his face, and disappears, leaving half of his rum St. James.

I stare at Lea. "I can't believe you see that shithead. Even went to Cannes with him."

Lea's face turns to granite. "Look," she says "we are not betrothed, you and I. We're friends that sometimes sleep together. If I choose to go to Cannes, or anywhere else, with someone, that's no business of yours."

"But with Dr. Cortisone, for Christ's sake. A shithead if I ever met one."

Lea comes to her feet and grabs her purse. "This conversation is over," she says and heads for the door.

I finish Vernon's rum; he's right, the stuff tastes like alcoholic piss. Probably been on the shelf too long. I stumble over the dog's paw on the way out; the animal lets out a yip. "Watch where you're bloody well going!" the man at the table exclaims in a British accent. The woman with him snatches the dog into her arms. "Poor Muldoon," she coos to the terrier's muzzle. "Did that mean beggar man hurt you?"

I catch up with Lea and grab her arm. She jerks it away. "Jealousy does not become you, Franklin," she says as she hustles down the boulevard while I march along beside her. After a block on high heels her walk slows. "Michael can be very interesting," she says. "Maybe a little stuffy, but he's knowledgeable about many things."

"I think he's a shithead all the same." My voice sounds petulant which is bad because it diminishes the effect.

Lea slows further then looks over at me and smiles, her teeth white and beautiful against her tan skin. "Maybe just a little," she says.

Sometimes I overhear Madame on the phone in the hallway. Most of the time she's talking to her daughter; she speaks to her in a voice very different from the one I'm accustomed to. Sometimes it's strident, aggressive, other times frustrated; it's never pleading. Virtually always the subject is money. She comes away from these conversations upset and needs to walk afterwards.

Street vendors are out now, selling roast chestnuts, peanuts, candied apples and oranges from carts. I've discovered that chestnuts are Madame's favorite and often I'll buy her a small bag, hurrying home so I can offer them to her while they're still fragrant and warm. Sometimes I present her with a more substantial gift: flowers, a book; once I found a silver pin in the form of a soaring bird in an antique shop on the Rue du Faubourg St. Honoré. It seemed to tie my novel and Mme Colmar together, and though it was expensive I bought it anyway. Madame was so pleased that she wore it for days afterwards, even around the house.

March 6. The young woman that François presented to me is very beautiful. Of course they are lovers. I could tell by the way he looked at her though I refrained from asking. She must be the woman he alluded to during one of our walks. I found something restless and dissatisfied about the girl, and her proposal to procure jewelry and art for me was disturbing. She impressed me as a charlatan, but a beautiful one and by her clothing I would say one who is doing quite well. François is intelligent and he can, I am certain, clearly discern what was obvious even in my brief encounter. Still, logic is always at the mercy of the heart, and he may be blind to her weakness of character or rationalize it in some way... I must be careful of jealousy. The other afternoon I made it a point to leave Mme de Hauteville earlier than usual and rush home. I had an overpowering suspicion that I would catch them together in François's bed. When he was not in his room I imagined them together elsewhere. Jealousy is nourished by doubt—I should ask him simply and directly what is his relation with this girl. He would never lie to me. But I must avoid the appearance *of jealousy, for while jealousy may cause me to suffer, I'm certain it will arouse little sympathy in François.*

The date approaches. I can hear *it approach. Sometimes it is a wind howling on a precipice, other times a roaring waterfall or a whistling shell. Yet when I focus on the day itself, all is still. The day appears as a limitless vista under a chalk sky, swamp-like to the horizon, its surface flecked with green clots. Then slowly, my body naked, I sink without struggle into the black ooze, the odor of tar filling my nostrils, until I am completely enveloped. There is no ripple on the swamp.*

I must remain clear-headed, not think of any of this. I have arranged for François to meet with Mme Parlanges the day after tomorrow.

10

The days are

longer. I stare out the window of my room; at midday, sunlight now brightens a corner of the garden; there are green patches but the lone scraggly tree is as dead-looking as ever. "Mme Parlanges would be pleased to meet you," Madame says at my door. "I took the liberty of arranging a rendezvous for tomorrow afternoon at three... We must be on time. To be late for an appointment with Mme Parlanges causes her to read all sorts of sinister intentions into the event... Incidentally, you may find her abrupt, even prying. Do not be insulted. It is the way she acquaints herself with people." The following day I wear my only suit; the pants, I notice, are now two sizes too large. I chalk this up to frugal eating, a long cold winter and the flu and experience a pleasant sense of artistic martyrdom.

The apartment of Mme Parlanges, on the Rue des Bernardins (in a neat brick building with a wrought iron balcony around each window), is larger than Mme Colmar's; in the watery March light that filters past the gauze curtains, the massive stuffed furniture, cabinets, tables and lamps that surround us take on the character of a protective wall, bulwarks against an uncertain world. The place has a vague perfume odor—I imagine little sachet packets filled with ground up lavender plants hidden in the furniture. I have an urge to open windows, let in fresh air. I expected Mme Parlanges to be thin, nervous, instead she's a heavy woman, swathed in yards of fabric, and, ensconced in a stuffed throne-like chair, looks like a suspicious Queen Victoria. She offers us Dubonnet and a plate of petit fours. "I have read excerpts of your Kinsey Report," Mme Parlanges says. "The author claims that 85 percent of American men have had sex before marriage and 50 percent are unfaithful. In France, I'm sure both of these figures would be 100 percent. But tell me, why are you people so preoccupied with these things? Why, like adolescents, are you obsessed with sexual affairs? And why this tendency to view man in the mass, as a statistic, as though we were discussing the size of cabbages, rather than individuals?"

I try my best. "Man in the mass is far more knowable than individuals," I say. "Besides, everyone is curious about the morals of his neighbor." Mme Parlanges watches me as I answer, eyes shrewd, intelligent.

Without visible transition, she goes on, "You are quite right in searching out and eliminating the Communists from your government. These people will not be satisfied until they have subjugated the world. They infiltrate everywhere. We French should follow your example... Tell me about yourself, *jeune homme*. What have you accomplished in your life? What are you most proud of? Where do you wish to go?"

I'm uncomfortable with this line of questioning, hesitate, take a swallow of Dubonnet, find it too sweet, occupy myself with the petit fours. Also too sweet. "I'm not a good student of my own life," I say. "To tell the truth I'm confused as to what I want to do. I came to Paris to find out whether I am a writer."

"And what have you concluded?"

"I'm still confused... I hope confusion is not my permanent state."

"It is proper at your age to be uncertain," Mme Parlanges says, "but it's also important to examine your motives. Mme Colmar tells me that you are an engineer. Why did you choose to change profession?"

I fumble around for an answer while Mme Parlanges's steady gaze never leaves my face; I have the feeling that she can see into my mind. Mme Colmar stares at me as well. Why did I choose to write? I was not aware of a conscious choice, only a need to escape—from engineering, Boston, my family, the breakup with Irene. And the opportunity to escape, to run off to Paris, had presented itself in the form of Lea and writing. I stare past Mme Parlanges and realize with full force how tightly bound these two were: I had sensed in Boston that it was the writing part of me that appealed to Lea and it was to please her that I started to write. But imperceptibly, here in Paris, the writing had taken on another purpose, and it is this purpose that I struggle to articulate to the unwavering eyes before me.

"I chose to write because it was a way to start over," I reply. "Perhaps by exploring my own life through fiction I would come to better understand myself."

"And what have you learned?"

I grope for words in French, not sure what comes out but trying to say this: "I have often been mindless, usually embarking on a course blindly, and rarely have I made a conscious choice. In writing my book I am also trying to examine my life and at last consider what I wish to make of myself. No matter how imperfectly I do this, it has to be better than not examining it at all."

"Why Paris? Why did you not stay where you were?"

"To see my past life and my country whole, from the outside, rather than try to discern its shape while immersed in it. Besides, it's an American tradition for writers to come to Paris."

"Whom do you most admire?"

I think of my mother but decide that's a perilous answer, hesitate, then become aware of a steady ticking sound, regular as a heartbeat. An enormous grandfather clock sits in the corner; its pendulum, visible through a glass door, is taller than Mme Colmar and terminates in a massive copper disk that reflects the light of the window in dull glints as it swings hypnotically from side to side. Except for the ticking clock, the room is absolutely still. "*Alors...*" Mme Parlanges says not unkindly, though her voice seems too loud.

"The great engineers of the Renaissance," I reply to the swinging disk. "Without motors or cranes, using only muscle power and their own ingenuity, they miraculously built the great cathedrals of Europe."

I turn to Mme Parlanges and see by the slight flicker of her eyelids that she finds this answer less than satisfying. She doesn't let up. It isn't that her manner is aggressive, just steady, unrelenting. "What are you ashamed of in your life?"

"My father," I say. It just comes out, surprising me, as though someone else had spoken through my mouth. I thought I was being guarded but this emerged unbidden.

"And why is that?"

I plunge on, turning back no longer possible. "Because he's weak, dull, unsuccessful. I don't think he's ever had an original thought in his head." I find my tone belligerent, as though to better justify the heretical thing I'm saying.

"And your mother, is she the opposite of these things?"

"Almost. Yes."

"Were you close to your mother?"

"Not always," I say and feel myself flailing in deep water. "I admire her patience, her ability to live with my father. He's a frail dreary man as well as a poor provider. She made a home for us out of thin air."

"What do you most fear?"

"Failure," I say. "Becoming like my father."

Mme Parlanges shakes her head. "Perhaps the poor man was simply unfortunate," she says.

"It's difficult to distinguish the unfortunate from the incompetent," I say, once again belligerent. I suspect it's the foreign language that makes the words less real and therefore sayable.

"Have you ever had a profound love affair?"

I think of Irene. I suppose our affair was "profound," at least for a while. "I had a love affair that ended in failure. Perhaps that's why I sometimes think of it as 'profound.'"

"Why did it fail?"

"It's difficult to say, difficult even to think about."

"I gather then that she left you."

"Yes, she did."

"And what did you learn from that experience?"

"I'm still trying to piece together what happened."

I become aware that my hands are cold; I have the impression that I'm being interviewed for a job by a tough personnel director, though I have no idea what the job is, and the man is going to keep at it until he has unraveled my past down to the details of toilet training.

Throughout our exchange Mme Parlanges has not changed position nor budged an inch, only kept her eyes trained on my face, and this immobility has contributed to her regal appearance, a venerable queen judging an accused subject. I'm tensed for another question when, mercifully,

Mme Colmar says, "Why did your President threaten to trounce a critic who found fault with his daughter's singing? That is after all a critic's role."

I try to beam gratitude at her with my eyes. "I think he was reacting as a father whose daughter had been insulted rather than as President," I say.

Mme Parlanges leans back in her throne chair, drains her Dubonnet, sighs. I gather the interrogation is over. "I suppose you can consider these the excesses of a young nation. Charming in a way. You must remember that we are more staid. We have, after all, been in existence a trifle longer. On July 8th Paris will be two thousand years old."

The precise date strikes me as suspect. "Why July 8th?" I ask.

"Because the weather should be nice," Mme Parlanges replies. "It's a practical matter. Why choose a day in February? Besides, it's a Sunday."

In whirligig fashion Mme Parlanges switches the subject to flying saucers and whether I believe we are indeed being visited by beings from other worlds.

Outside, I comment, "Mme Parlanges should have been a lawyer. I felt my whole life pried open for inspection. There seemed to be no reasonable limit to her curiosity."

"You must not take her inquisitiveness as a personal affront," Madame says. "This is her bent. The who, what, and where of things most interest her. She would have made an excellent novelist. Issues and events concern her only to the extent they reveal human nature. People are her interest—and she does not believe, as you could perceive from her questions, that they act out of simple motives. She constantly searches for double meanings, things hidden. It can be very exasperating."

I don't find her apology for Mme Parlanges's interrogation convincing. "But there was more than that," I say. "Her questions were an examination of sorts... as though

I were on trial."

Madame laughs. "You are becoming European, François. Suspicion is our natural state." We are at the intersection with the Boulevard St. Germain and Madame comments on the delicate filigree of metal and glass on the tower that caps the rear of the church of St. Nicolas across the street.

The following afternoon, as I sip Cointreau with Mme Colmar, she keeps adjusting the doily on the coffee table and, something most unusual, raises her voice at M. Colmar. "Stop eating! For the love of God, stop eating. You'll turn into a whale." The old man looks more confused than ever and wanders out of the room.

I pick up Madame's copy of *Figaro*. There is a photograph of Julius and Ethel Rosenberg, on trial for passing atomic secrets to the Russians, on the front page. His hands are clasped but handcuffs are just visible at the wrists, his soft round face is hardened by a precise mustache, light reflects off his thin-framed glasses; he looks like a high school science teacher about to answer an easy question. Ethel's hands are hidden; her pudgy face, black button eyes and pursed mouth give her a schoolteacher appearance as well—a fussy martinet running a class of fourth graders; she seems quite satisfied with herself, as though she has just said something clever. I have the impression they both feel morally superior. "They deserve to be put to death," Madame says unemotionally. "Betrayal of any trust is despicable but to betray one's own country..."

"I suspect they thought they were accomplishing some greater good," I say.

Madame waves this away as a non sequitur, then is silent. She seems to be struggling with something. "A date is approaching," she finally says, and once again adjusts the doily. She hesitates again then rises and goes to the window and opens the curtains. "The seventeenth of April," she says to the window, "the anniversary of Mme de Sévigné's death."

"Is that important?" I ask her lighted silhouette.

She moves away from the window and I can now see her face; she seems appalled, as though I had questioned the existence of a divine Providence. "Well, yes," she says. "Our lives have paralleled in so many ways, including the day and month of our birth, that it's difficult to believe that our deaths will not coincide as well." She says this as though she is stating the obvious to a deficient child.

"Permit me, Madame, to say that's ridiculous!" pops out despite me. I know I should be more respectful of her superstitions.

"Things you believe are never ridiculous," Madame says. "I have consulted the tarot hundreds of times and in one fashion or another, sometimes stronger and other times weaker, with differing symbols, the cards are always in agreement with this prediction. It is easy to ridicule them."

I sigh and have the feeling that I'm arguing with someone about religion.

Mme Colmar returns to her accustomed place and leans toward me. "This story will interest you," she says, "doubting Thomas that you are. One week before we left on holiday to Honfleur, thirty-six years ago, I consulted a tarot reader. I have played the episode over in my mind a thousand times and can bring it forth at will, as though it occurred this morning. The reader was a woman of about my age at the time, black hair and one eye cast to the side, her fingers long and hands slender, quite sensual actually. She wore a perfume that I have never again encountered. She asked that I shuffle the cards, then that I shuffle them again. I had to repeat this at least ten times before she was satisfied. The first card, laid in the center of the table, was The Fool, at least that's what it is called. In that deck The Fool was a youth, dressed in a gold and red tunic, head lifted heavenward, holding aloft a white rose; he was advancing toward a precipice, blue waves beneath, a dog barking at his feet. The second card, placed across The Fool, was The High Priestess. She wore a blue-white gown, its folds a shimmering radiance, like moonlight on water, that flowed out of the picture. The Fool was upside down to me and The High Priestess sideways, but the next card faced me. A knight in armor rode upon a white horse; he had trampled a fallen king and drew near to a woman and child who turned from him, huddled in dread. The knight carried a banner on which was a five-petaled rose, white against a red background. A river coursed behind him. It was only after the other cards were on the table that I noticed the face of the knight: it was a skull, black sockets for eyes and nose, teeth grinning; the hands that held the reins were skeleton bones." Madame recounted all this as though the cards were unfolding before her at that very moment.

"You have transformed this episode into a permanent nightmare," I say.

Madame pays no attention to my remark as she continues. "When I told the woman we were about to leave for the seaside, she quickly pointed out two other cards, the nine of swords—a woman awakening in the dead of night, head in her hands, nine swords hanging menacingly above her head—and the five of cups—a bent figure wrapped in a black cloak contemplating five spilled cups upon the ground—and took my hands in hers and implored me not to go.

"I related all this to my husband—I recall the anxiety in my voice as I repeated the woman's admonition—but he found it all very amusing and laughed and chuckled as he packed his bag... Of course, he didn't laugh or chuckle when our son drowned."

I can see that her mesmerizing belief in the cards is

unshakable, nevertheless I try, a little wearily but I try. "Many anniversaries of de Sévigné's death have come and gone, Madame, but you are still among the living."

"I realize that, yet each year as the date of her death approaches, I'm always apprehensive. And when it passes uneventfully I always feel great relief, as though Providence has granted me another year of life."

"I'm sure this one will pass uneventfully as well. You're still a youthful and vibrant woman."

"You are very kind, François, but this anniversary is different." I now see that she's genuinely frightened. "This time I shall be the same age as Mme de Sévigné was at her death." Her voice is suddenly hoarse. "Worse. Last night I had a nightmare, a vision of my own coffin being lowered into a grave, and watched the first clods soundlessly strike the wood. Poor Gustave, wearing a tattered suit and looking like The Hermit in an ancient tarot deck, stared down without comprehension. My daughter Berthe, a smirk on her face, was satisfied at last."

"It was only a bad dream, brought on by your apprehension over the coming anniversary."

"But there was something else. When I awoke, I felt I was suffocating and rushed to the window and flung it open, to breathe the outside air. It was early morning, the sky just brightening, and in the dim light the tree in the garden resembled a dark skull. I then heard a terrible cawing sound and espied a crow perched on the outermost branch. He sat there, sleek and fat, an augur of death."

I touch her hand and try to help by quoting Saint Augustine. "Though all signs are things, not all things are signs." But Mme Colmar's eyes are fixed elsewhere and her face appears confused. I can see she isn't listening. The seventeenth of April will be in five weeks.

March 9. I did not broach the purpose of our visit to

Mme Parlanges, only that I wanted her assessment of the young man. (Were I to reveal the idea to her or to Mme de Hauteville, they would consider me insane.) Mme Parlanges found François forthright, honest, somewhat troubled. But then who of us is not troubled in some way? And who of us is not puzzled by himself? I thought he acquitted himself well under difficult circumstances. Perhaps I should have let her continue, but the poor boy appeared so uncomfortable that I had to interrupt. Besides, I had heard enough. He has had his difficulties like the rest of us and borne them reasonably well. Did any of this give me greater insight, a better grasp whether the idea is worthwhile? Perhaps—at least I have Mme Parlanges's appraisal of François. I promised myself not to depend on intuition or a burst of insight, but to evaluate the idea rationally. I shall think of this further...

March 10. I could not contain myself and told François of the approaching date. I felt it as an increasing heaviness upon me, too great a burden to bear alone and, on the impulse of the moment, decided to share it with him. I could see sympathy in his splendid brown eyes but also a skeptical look, as though this were only a temporary madness and would, like a headache or a cut finger, soon heal itself. Still, I do feel relieved that he now knows what lies before me. For I can now speak openly to him of the date and this thought gives me solace.

I look up the age of Mme de Sévigné at her death: she was seventy. It occurs to me that Mme Colmar's mother was a contemporary of Abraham Lincoln. I find the thought beyond belief. That night in bed Madame huddles close to me as though seeking protection. "I feel a cold coming on," she says. "I have always had a fragile chest. These things, you know, can easily lead to pneumonia."

"I think you need distraction," I say. "Why don't I take

you to Versailles. It's almost spring, some flowers might already be out. We can stroll in the gardens, enjoy the sunshine. The tourist season hasn't started so it should not be crowded."

"That's a marvelous idea," Madame says. "We can leave early and be back in plenty of time for M. Colmar's dinner."

"Let's go tomorrow," I say. Getting away from my book is to me the most appealing aspect of the idea.

In the chateau my eye is continually drawn away from the paintings, sculptures and gilded scrollwork that cover the walls and ceilings to the windows and the sunshine reflecting off the pools and the garden outside. Madame must feel the same pull because she moves quickly through the various rooms toward the exit (pausing only to observe that the dominant color everywhere, as befits a king, is gold). We both slow in the sunshine and meander through the parterres in front of the castle: the shrubs are cut low and arranged in arabesque patterns punctuated by conical evergreens.

We sit on a bench near the central fountain. After the icy winter, spring seems to be early; the warm sun soaks through me, makes me somnolent. I gaze at the white marble statue of a woman sheltering two children, eyes cast heavenward, atop the fountain; she's surrounded by frogs, each with his mouth open, ready to spew a jet of water. "The woman is Latona," Madame explains. "Her two children are Diana and Apollo. The figures around them are peasants who scorned Latona and were turned by Jupiter into frogs." Madame smiles. "Never scorn the gods, François," she says.

I try to take in the enormous expanse of castle, awed by the scale of it. Then I think of the great king. "I suspect Louis XIV was something of a megalomaniac," I say. "In building this place he wanted to create a monument in keeping with his view of himself."

Madame shakes her head. "You cannot use today's vocabulary of character analysis to comprehend an absolute monarch of the 17th century," she says. "His was an age in which one considered posterity. In building Versailles, the king looked beyond his own time. He knew that nothing marks the greatness of a nation or the glory of an epoch more than the monuments it leaves behind. Louis XIV built Versailles not as a monument to himself, but rather to the France of his reign, a very different thing." She says this in a positive way, sure of herself, but without aggressiveness, then seems to relax and lose interest in the Sun King.

I become aware of other fountains around us and say, "It must be dazzling when the water jets are playing." Then, growing extravagant in the blessed sunshine, "The most glorious place on earth."

We are silent for a while, adrift in the sun, then Madame turns toward me: her face, particularly her forehead, seems oddly naked and innocent; sunlight illuminates the irises of her eyes—feathery blue-grey shapes float toward the black pool in the center—for the first time I'm aware of her eye color. I take her hand and we sit this way, motionless as lizards on a rock, gazing past the tended gardens across a long avenue of green to another basin where golden horses pull a chariot through the water—a canal beyond stretches toward the horizon and the light blue of the sky. I don't know how long we sat there, surrounded by Versailles, by history, time transformed into space.

A woman of about Mme Colmar's age is seated on a nearby bench. She too appears stunned by the sun; she gazes straight ahead and seems to be thinking profoundly about nothing at all. When we leave I notice that she's carrying an umbrella. "Are you expecting rain?" I ask, pointing to the clear sky.

"Rheumatism plagues my life," she says, something final and sad in her voice. "I need a cane to walk but a cane makes me appear old."

"I give thanks that Providence has spared me these ailments," Madame says to me as we move away. A workman in a light green uniform rakes a garden path, leaving it evenly rippled, like corduroy.

We stroll along the walkways. Stone statues of curly-bearded muscular men and bare-breasted women, illuminated by the sun, stand out sharp white against the dark trees. I imagine receptions, parties, theater, fireworks, and women with slender waists and bouffant skirts being stalked by men with buckle shoes. Madame pauses before a bed of violets growing in the shadow of an evergreen. The rich purple flowers tilt downward. "When I was a child," she says, "my grandmother told me that these violets grew in the shade of the cross, and since then droop their heads in sorrow."

On our return I notice the woman from the bench moving slowly along a path in the garden; the tip of her umbrella leaves dents in the carefully raked ground.

At Madame's suggestion we lunch at *Au Chapeau Gris*. She studies the menu, face serious. "What we eat is always so important to you," I say.

Madame stares at me, still serious. "Of course it is important, my dear François. Eating is more than taking nourishment. We do not eat only to live, or for that matter make love only to procreate, or seek a roof only for shelter. The way we do these things reflects our aesthetic sensibility and sets us apart from animals." She returns to the menu. "They are, at bottom, celebrations of life."

An elderly lady beside us is dining alone. Periodically she glances at me. She has a wicker basket beside her from which a dog occasionally peers out. She feeds the animal a scrap of food then looks up and notices Mme Colmar observing her. "His name is Anicet," she says and lifts the creature out of the basket and holds him in her gemmed hands, muzzle close to her face. He's fluffy brown, the fur around his mouth black, nose pink flecked with black, bulging eyes; he looks like he has a thyroid problem. The woman kisses Anicet and he licks her mouth. "The day after tomorrow is his birthday," she says. "As a treat, I'll take him to a bordello for dogs near the Pont de Passy." She wiggles the dog before her. "You would like that, wouldn't you, *petit cochon*," she says. Anicet licks her face in appreciation. The woman shoves the little guy back in the basket and feeds him another scrap. She looks at me. "Your son is a handsome young man," she says.

"Oh, he's not my son," Mme Colmar says. The woman stares at me appraisingly. Some secret communication seems to have passed between the two women. "You are very fortunate," the woman with the dog says. She appears to be speaking to both of us. Mme Colmar slips me money to pay the check.

On the train back to Paris, while I'm still marveling at the bordello for dogs, she says, "That woman would no doubt like to share you with me. By the look of her, I have no doubt that she would treat you handsomely."

"That's a horrible thought," I say, identifying with Anicet.

Madame pats my hand and stares out the window; houses roofed in red tile and stone fences and countryside give way to squat brick manufacturing buildings and closely packed gray tenements. I sense Madame's thoughts returning to Mme de Sévigné. I'm thinking of something else: it finally occurs to me why I was depressed after the ice cream episode—I have become a gigolo.

11

The sun is wonderfully warm as Lea and I sit in the square in front of the church of St. Sulpice and idly watch an old woman on a nearby bench, dressed in a heavy coat as though it were still the depth of winter, feed morsels of bread to the pigeons. The grass forms islands of green. There is the pleasant splash of water in the fountain in the center of the square. I take off my sweater. Lea stares at me and frowns. "Where did you get that shirt?" she asks.

It's a light tan silk. Madame said the instant she saw it, she thought of my eyes and knew it was for me. "Mme Colmar gave it to me."

"That's strange. What else has she given you?"

"Knickknacks. Little things." I suddenly feel guilty and look up at the fountain: it's a three-tiered affair, two crouching stone lions on each side, jaws open, pigeons on their heads, a coiled bronze serpent in the flow of water.

"Why would she do that? You're just a boarder. Why would she spend money on you?"

"I think she likes me. We sit around, chat, sometimes take a walk together. I suspect she's grateful for the company." This questioning is not like Lea; I can see she's in a bitchy mood.

"One of the pharmacists panicked," Lea finally says.

"What happened?"

"A woman who took our cortisone started to grow a mustache and her features swelled. The pharmacist said he hardly recognized her when she came in. Her face looked like a full moon. Then she claims her vision's blurred. She's convinced there's poison in the drug. Anyway, she threatened to go to the police unless the pharmacist returned her money."

"I suspect he returned the money."

"Sure. What else would he do? He returned the money and now he wants it back from me."

"What did you tell him?"

"I told him fine. He'll have the money in the morning. Let him find me... Then there's another problem."

"Don't tell me, let me guess. Everyone that's taken the drug is inflating like a blowfish."

"Almost. Another pharmacist said a woman complained of swollen hands and legs, fast heartbeat, stomach pains, insomnia... all kinds of problems. What really bothered her though were the swollen legs. Her husband always thought her legs were the most exciting thing about her."

"So much for the benign and natural drug... Does she want her money back too?"

"No. The druggist told her about the young student who imports the drug from Switzerland. All she wants to do is find me and scratch my eyes out... I called Michael. He said it probably has something to do with dosage or frequency."

"Was he worried? I mean it would be awkward if

somebody died."

Lea glances at me, face startled; I don't think that thought ever occurred to her. "Don't be morbid, for Christ's sake."

"Well, was Michael concerned?" I couldn't keep the sarcasm out of my voice as I said Michael.

"No, he didn't seem worried. In fact, he talked to me like *I* was the patient. As though *I* had the problem. Told me not to get hysterical, but to stop selling until we see what happens to the rest of the people who took the drug."

"It's a new medicine," I say. "I doubt if our enterprising little doctor understands it."

"Don't defend the son of a bitch," Lea says morosely. "I took all the risk and he made all the money... But you're right, he's not worried. For him it's just a business that ran into trouble." Lea lapses into gloom.

"Now what?"

"He's onto another drug. An anti-morning sickness thing for pregnant women. He says we're a great team and could make a fortune on this one."

"What did you tell him?"

"To go screw himself."

"Good answer."

"I've turned off the subagents. Told them the supply dried up. We're already in enough of a mess."

The overcoated woman has exhausted her supply of bread and the pigeons bob off; the woman, elbows on her knees, back bent, a melancholy expression on her face, watches the ungrateful pigeons leave. She sits motionless, stylized like an old engraving. Lea watches the pigeons as well. I've never seen Lea so down. I think of her huge investment in the cortisone business—all that running around, convincing, creating miraculous success where there was nothing—exploding like a grenade in her face. And her partner shrugging it off as though it were a little rain at a Sunday picnic.

"I've started going to classes again," Lea says. This seems to depress her further. We sit without saying anything. I notice a black insect emerge from a crack in the pavement, test the air with his feelers, then scuttle across the concrete and disappear into another crack. Lea takes my hand. "Thanks for your help, Franklin." There are tears in her eyes. We hold hands and gaze at the fountain; there's a rainbow in the water.

"Why don't we wander over to your place?" I say.

She stares at me, mouth tightening. Lousy timing. "Christ, there must be something on your mind besides getting laid," she says. "Anyway, why my place? I thought you didn't like my place. What about *your* place?"

"I'd be glad to take you to my room," I say, trying to recover. "It's just that Mme Colmar is so rigid about no female visitors. The place is cheap, you know, and convenient. I wouldn't want to get thrown out... Besides, you wouldn't like it. It's dilapidated."

"Let's go anyway," she says, voice firm. "It's not like we're going to throw a party." I can see that Lea badly needs a win and she's not going to yield on this.

I study the façade of St. Sulpice; the structure suddenly seems important to me. What strikes me is its weight— thick columns, no windows, massive towers at either end— all devoid of ornament, nothing to lighten the mass of stone. "You know, that's an ugly building," I finally say.

"Why does it take so much courage for you to decide a simple thing?" Lea says.

I continue to stare at the church: columns support a monumental balcony—how nice it would be if a robed figure appeared there and blessed all living things in the square, including the pigeons and the insects. Then, reluctantly, finding no way out and smelling disaster, I sigh and at last say, "All right, but we can't go today. Why don't we make it tomorrow afternoon. That way you'll see the place in daylight." The following day, I realized, is Thursday and should be safe: Madame is usually visiting Mme de Hauteville. The night is out of the question since Madame is now in the habit of kissing me good night before going to bed or spending the night in my room.

When we leave, sunlight brightens the serpent in the fountain: it's tarnished a uniform green, the same color those cheap rings and bracelets leave your skin.

The following morning I tidy up my room and try to distract myself by reading the newspaper. *Le Monde* predicts that Julius and Ethel Rosenberg will be found guilty and sentenced to death and is already indignant over this. In her cell, in the Federal Court House in New York City, Ethel was heard singing "Good Night Irene." Julius was more serious: he sang "The Battle Hymn of the Republic."

I take Lea to the Rue Danton and check that Madame is truly gone while Lea waits in the hall. When I'm satisfied, I slip her into my room. "For heaven's sake, stop acting as though we're a pair of thieves," Lea says, too loud I thought. She looks around. "Well it's not bad. Small, but neat... and you have a little closet and a sink... and a garden no less."

I find Lea silhouetted against the window, here in my room, exciting. I put my arms around her, fondle her breasts, and move her toward my bed.

Afterward we lie together and Lea stares up at the flaking ceiling. "You're right," she says. "This place *is* dilapidated."

"It's too bad," I say, "because the old lady deserves better. And her husband, well, he's senile now but apparently was an exceptional mathematician."

"Any children?"

"One daughter, like her idol, Mme de Sévigné. But their

relationship is not the best."

Lea continues to stare up at the ceiling, hands clasped behind her head. "The short and simple annals of the poor," she says. "I can see your landlady isn't in the market for diamonds or Renoirs or Monets. I was wasting my breath."

Then, perhaps to get Lea's attention or to raise Mme Colmar's standing in Lea's eyes, I say, "You know, she has in the house letters written by Mme de Sévigné to one of Mme Colmar's ancestors." Like a musician who has just played a false note, hears it float off into the air, wrong and irretrievable, I hear my own words, profoundly and irretrievably wrong.

Lea turns toward me. "She has what?"

As in the interrogation by Mme Parlanges, I can no longer turn back. "Eight letters written by de Sévigné to a great-great-grand something of Mme Colmar's."

Lea sits up and leans forward, her breasts close to me. "You mean they're in this apartment?"

"Yes, right here in this apartment."

"Where?"

"I haven't any idea where, but I'm sure they're well-hidden." I lick the nipple of Lea's adjacent breast, trying to distract her.

"Do you realize that you have our salvation within your reach?"

"What are you saying?" I ask her breast though I know very well what she's saying.

She raises the sheet between her body and my face. "Don't act stupid, Frank. The old fool possesses a fortune that she's never cashed in and never will, otherwise she wouldn't live this way." Lea nods toward the room. "Or take in boarders. Those letters have probably been hidden in the same place for years. If you took the letters, she'd never miss them."

"I wouldn't call Mme Colmar a fool," I say.

"All right, call her anything you want," Lea says, her voice rising with impatience.

"Look, I have no interest in stealing Mme Colmar's letters, or anything else. I'm sorry I brought the subject up."

"Do you have any idea how much those things are worth?"

"I have no idea," I say. Though I'm struggling to make the subject disappear, it continues to enlarge and I realize that by the way I've said the words I have invited an answer.

"In the tens of thousands of dollars, I'm sure," Lea says.

"You'd never be able to sell them," I say, though I have no idea what I'm talking about.

Lea drops the sheet and shakes her head in a rapid impatient gesture. "Don't concern yourself with that. Just get the letters. I'll worry about selling them." Her nipples protrude from their delicate brown areoles and stare at me. "Have you *seen* the letters?" she asks.

"No, Mme Colmar just told me she has them."

"Well, you have to see them. This may all be the idle chatter of an addled old lady."

We're still naked together in bed and I'm both reflecting on my own stupidity and feeling the stirring of desire when the door opens. It's Mme Colmar, home early.

Madame stares at the two of us, her face surprisingly satisfied, as though she's been trying to solve a puzzle and suddenly knows the solution. Then her eyes narrow and her mouth tightens. "This is not a bordello," she says. I expected her to shout, to be indignant, but her voice is solid, business-like, similar to her daughter's when I overheard them arguing.

Apparently Madame recognizes Lea. "I knew it would be you," she says. "I *thought* you were a *putain* when I met you. I can see that I was right." Her voice is even, without discernible anger. I have never seen so much dignity nor have I ever felt so tender toward her as I do now. She fastens her gaze on me. "Why did you bring a whore into my house?" Then suddenly the dignity is gone and her face fractures as she screams, "How dare you bring a whore into my house!"

I jump at the scream but Lea, in a steady voice, sounding not at all defensive but perplexed, says, "Why are you so upset, Madame? Even if I am a whore what difference does it make to you? Who your boarder sleeps with is no affair of yours." She says this as she gets out of bed.

Madame does not respond, her face a tight mask, her figure stiff and perfectly erect. She crosses her arms and surveys Lea's body; the tan has remained, setting off the white of Lea's lovely ass. As Lea dresses, M. Colmar, bathrobe awry, appears at the door, looks around in his lost way, then helps himself to a chunk of chocolate from my dresser.

"Are you coming with me?" Lea says in English.

Madame apparently understands because she says, "If you leave now, you need not bother to return." Her mouth is a thin tight line and her eyes never waver but appear to sink deeper into their dark hollows.

"You had best stay and tranquillize your landlady," Lea says. Then to my astonishment she holds out her hands toward Mme Colmar, palms up, and says in a soft voice, "Forgive us, Madame. We meant no harm." I can see that her thoughts have returned to the Sévigné letters. She slips past the old man, who is now munching on my chocolate, and is gone.

Madame's face does not change but her voice is puzzled. "Did you *want* me to find you here... with another woman... in this bed where we have made love? You're not a sadistic man. Why did you do this?"

I sit up in bed. There is no answer other than my own stupidity. Then, with the precision of an engineering drawing, I recall the black and pink muzzle and the thyroid eyes peering out of the wicker basket in the restaurant in Versailles. A kept thing. Someone's property. "I can sleep with whoever I want, whenever I want," I say in a clipped voice. "You do not own me. Besides, this is my room. I pay for it. The next time you want to enter, please knock." I start to dress.

The rigidity in her face slowly comes apart, her body sags, and she looks down. I'm about to put on my undershirt when she says in a calm voice, "Thank you so much for staying." She comes close to me, something of the penitent child about her. "Please hold me," she says. She hugs my body, head against my naked chest. "You must answer my question, François. It is important to me."

I hold her at arms length and stare into her face, anger gone. "It was a foolish thing to do. We wanted to make love and had nowhere else to go. It's as simple as that." There are tears in Madame's eyes and I hug her to me. "I'm sorry," I say.

She kisses my chest. "In time you will understand what it means to be vulnerable."

She watches me finish dressing, then says as she leaves the room, "Examine your motives carefully, François. Your answer is *too* simple, *too* naive. Look into your heart and tell me what you find."

How did I get into this mess? I ask myself.

In the late morning of the following day Madame shows up with a small rectangular box. "A gift," she says, "to remind you who you are." Inside I find a bracelet, a flat silver bar and chain, the name François engraved in the bar.

"You're a whore," Lea says clinically. "All that fuss was the outrage of a jealous woman, not an upset landlady. You've been fornicating with her, haven't you?" She watches my face and when I don't answer she says, "You give me lectures on theft, morality, selling illegal drugs, even tell me I plagiarized my thesis. But you're a gigolo, peddling your body to a hundred-year-old lady... Besides buying you shirts, how much does she pay you?"

"She doesn't pay me anything," I say. But under Lea's skeptical gaze I feel both guilty and pissed. "Anyway, my relationship with Mme Colmar is none of your goddamned business."

I now see that Lea's face is relaxed and there is no anger in her. It's as though some business side of her has been working. She pays no attention to my response, looks beyond me, then abruptly says, "There are only two questions: do the Sévigné letters really exist in that apartment and if the answer is yes, how do we get our hands on them?"

"I can't possibly steal those letters," I say with finality.

"Why not? Don't tell me you feel tender toward your client... But let's do things in their proper order. First find out if the letters exist,"—she takes on a coy expression—"François."

"Don't call me that!"

"You're right. That's your *nom de travail*. Only old ladies can call you that."

"Why are you badgering me over Mme Colmar?" I say, pissed again. "I told you a minute ago—she's none of your fucking business."

"Okay. You're right." Lea holds up her hands in a conciliatory gesture, the same one she used with Mme Colmar. "It isn't any of my business." She smiles at me, a beautiful smile. "Is it too much to ask that you try to get a peek at those letters?... By the way, I like your mustache. It's very French."

March 17. François admitted that in bringing the girl to his room there may have been a subconscious desire to be

129

discovered. The reason being that he wished to assert his independence. I do not find the answer wholly satisfying but believe it is the best he can do. His indiscretion and the shallowness of his explanation has caused me to reevaluate the idea. Perhaps, as he said to Mme Parlanges, he is confused. (I must confess, out of his confusion arises a certain spontaneity, action not eroded by an excess of reflection, which I enjoy.) Still, at times I sense a certain emptiness in François, his character not completely formed. Perhaps this is a characteristic of America, the mutability of the new world. More likely he is still immature. Time and error should improve his judgement but I cannot be certain of this. I have set the idea aside for the time being.

Precisely one month remains. I must focus on the letters. I avoid this but it has to be done quickly. It is far easier to be wise for others than for oneself. I must find the courage to visit Berthe. Perhaps some new solution will occur to me seeing Berthe in her own milieu.

12

March 21.

I finally overcame my antipathy and visited Berthe in Orléans. The shop is on the Faubourg Bannier, near the Caserne Coligny, certainly not the fashionable part of the city. The place was awash in taffetas and moirés, tulles and chiffons, mostly in pink, blue and lavender, piled on the cutting table in a frozen tide of color. Two young women work at ancient treadle sewing machines in the back of the store, where there is also a range for cooking. The place smelled of cotton dust, perspiration, heated grease. Berthe treated the girls with great courtesy as she pointed out errors, corrections needed. I thought I discerned fleeting touches—of hair, neck, arms. One girl pricked her finger with a sewing needle and Berthe held her hand, stared at the wound, helped her bathe it in water.

Three customers came in for fittings while I was there. Berthe never presented me—I may as well have been the

131

cleaning woman or one of the girls rocking a treadle. I am no longer sure why I went; I suppose it was to observe Berthe more closely, hoping to find a ray of insight as I grope for a solution.

We had lunch at a nearby brasserie. After inquiring into Gustave's health and a complaint about the lack of business for Easter (my God, I can't believe that Easter Sunday is only four days off!), Berthe stared into the street, at the soldiers on bicycles returning to the caserne and the bourgeois hurrying toward whatever one does in Orléans. "Why have you come here, maman?" she asked.

"To visit with you, get out of my prison for a day. Spend a few moments with my own daughter... Am I not welcome?"

"Yes, you are always welcome. But I have learned that you do not spend time with me willingly. So when you do visit I wonder if there isn't something else, something you want... Is there anything else?"

"No. I am not here to beg for money or ask for favors of any kind. Only to see my daughter." When I said this I could see skepticism in her too steady stare and the tightness of her face.

Our food arrived; Berthe ate quickly, disgusting grey sausages with fried potatoes. A silence extended itself; two strangers sharing a table would have had more to say. "Why can we not speak to each other?" I ask in frustration.

"Because no matter what the subject may be," Berthe said, "it will always finish that you are a victim."

"But I am a victim," I said, trying at least by the force of my voice to make her comprehend.

"So is everyone," Berthe replied. "So am I. But I do not hammer you on the head with this. I accept what I am and make the best of things. Why can't you do the same?"

"But that is precisely what I try to do. Make the best of a miserable life."

"That is not true, maman. You try to lead a life beyond your means. And you do it at my expense."

"Ah, we are back to money... No! I refuse to speak of this. Tell me what you think of our new prime minister, of de Lattre in Indochina, of the Prix Goncourt. Tell me anything. But do not speak to me of money."

"These affairs do not concern me. I think very little of events I cannot change."

"What does concern you then? What is there in this wasteland of Orléans that excites you?"

Berthe hesitated, stared at her plate. "Is this a question of genuine interest to you?" she asked without raising her head.

"Of course. Why would I ask if it were not of interest to me?"

"I would like to prove Fermat's last theorem," she said to the remains of her sausages.

"You would like to do what?"

"Prove Fermat's last theorem. Papa struggled with this all of his life and never succeeded." She studied her plate. "I would like to accomplish this in his memory. I have his notebooks and have been studying them and working on this for almost four years. Finally it is clear to me where he went astray." She looked up at me: her eyes were bright and for an instant her face took on a kind of beatitude, a rapture, that I had never before seen in her. She bolted the rest of her food. "I must return to the shop," she said without looking at me.

I straightened the racks, arranged the fabrics, the clothes dummies, threads, needles, all the loose things lying about. As we finally pecked each other's cheek I suppressed a sigh of relief and hurried out the door. I felt as though I were leaving a plague-stricken house.

Waiting for the train, in the chill of late afternoon, I

became aware of a man who continued to stare at me. He was sturdy, capable looking, not unattractive, his hair thick, pepper-and-salt in color; he carried no briefcase and was casually dressed. "Forgive me for staring," he said, "but I am an amateur art historian and your face bears an extraordinary resemblance to a little known portrait by El Greco, the Mater Dolorosa, in the Strasbourg museum. Perhaps it is your blue shawl that contributes to the likeness..."

"That's the most charming approach I have experienced since I was a young woman."

He smiled, teeth even, his own. The only defect a mashed nose, giving him the appearance of a damaged Greek sculpture. "But it's true, chère Madame. *If you are ever in Strasbourg..."*

He introduced himself as Matthieu Jaubert; we chatted of art (he too loved Vermeer's The Lace Maker *and said his idea of paradise would be to spend eternity in the Uffizi gallery in Florence) and politics and the fate of France and the fate of the world. There was a virile manly odor about him. "A pity to break off this conversation simply because the train has reached its destination," he said at the Gare d'Orléans. "Would you care to join me for dinner? I know of an excellent brasserie nearby."*

Well, I had left a stew on the stove for Gustave and the company was most agreeable... At the restaurant Jaubert ordered Pernod then a bottle of Montrachet. As we drank our apéritif there was a subtle but steady shift in authority: Jaubert took charge of the meal, the conversation, and something covetous crept into his gaze. He placed his hand on mine, a sure commanding hand. I found none of this unpleasant and when we sipped our coffee and cognac and he said it was a pity to say good night and he knew of a congenial hotel nearby, I readily acquiesced.

Jaubert had rather odd sexual practices but they were

not displeasing. I must confess there is something satisfying about sex with a stranger, to concentrate completely on one's own pleasure, knowing that there is no sequel, no need for life together to continue afterward. We had breakfast in bed and sex a final time. In the intimate moment afterward, I decided to share with him my dream of the previous night. The dream had disturbed me and I thought that by speaking of it I might dissipate its effect. The dream was of my great uncle Albéric, the stonecutter. "He was a slow heavy man with huge hands, whose breath was a cloud of garlic," I said to the naked Jaubert beside me. "When I was a child he sometimes took me to his atelier, a dusty place where he and two assistants hewed marble into headstones. I remember the graceful angels and roses and doves and lambs these grey men carved into the polished surfaces. At the time I did not understand that the names on the stones were of those already dead, instead I thought of Uncle Albéric as god-like, deciding with his chisel who lived and who died... Last night I dreamt of him, back bent, alone in his shop, traversed by a shaft of light, slowly and irrevocably chipping my name into grey stone."

Jaubert yawned, rose, glanced at his watch, said he had to hurry to his apartment to change. He had a business meeting to attend and did not wish to be late. He asked for my address and phone number and I answered by taking his.

When I returned to the Rue Danton, François seemed concerned over my absence. I told him, managing a casual air, that I had spent the night with a man. "Oh," was all he said, and appeared distressed. This, I must admit, gave me pleasure.

March 23. François's love-making was particularly ardent last night. The classic style, I have to say, is for me the most satisfying.

It has been almost four months since Mme Colmar mentioned the Sévigné letters, but it seems like decades. She speaks of many things but never again brings up the letters. After the moment of obsession in the museum, whenever the letters resurfaced in my mind I experienced a sensation similar to peering down from a great height and shoved the thought away. But Lea's insistence that I see the letters, which after all only echoes my own curiosity, now weighs on me. I think back to Madame's words—confounded as they are with fever, bitter teas, strange pills—and they seem to float, like the letters themselves, in some distant void, fractured shapes like those cubist paintings where one searches for familiar objects among the kaleidoscopic surfaces. I tell myself that under no circumstances would I steal the letters, yet now when I look around the house I find to my surprise that it is with the eyes of a thief: I inspect the floor, the woodwork, the furniture, for secret cavities, concealed chambers where the letters may be hidden. When I catch myself doing this I shake my head in disgust—I'm not about to steal anything, certainly not from Mme Colmar.

One evening I'm surprised to find that Mme Colmar has arranged piles of clothing—dresses, sweaters, hats, gloves, shoes—in the *salon.* "What are you doing?" I ask.

"When I'm gone my daughter will only sell all this," she says. "I may as well give it to those who can make use of it."

For the first time the depth of Mme Colmar's identification with Mme de Sévigné and her belief that she will indeed die on the precise date of Sévigné's death, becomes concrete for me. "If you're wrong, you'll be left with nothing," I say.

She shakes her head rapidly, emphatically. "You may believe me, François, I am not wrong." I can tell by the finality with which she says this that further argument is hopeless.

Each morning Madame loads a canvas shopping bag

with the rags now piled on the carpet in the *salon* and disappears. One morning she asks me to accompany her. The sky is cloudless and the sun warm; on the streets everyone follows their *bonjour* with a smile and a comment on the weather; they all seem pleased with their lives. I carry two bags of clothing as we head toward the Seine. "I'm looking for the *clochards*," she says. "These people, you know, are not really vagrants or beggars—they remain a mystery to me and I'm not sure what they are. They disappear in winter like migrant birds but reappear in spring. They carry no *carte d'identité* and have no address. Mme Parlanges says that some are doctors or lawyers or businessmen who prefer an anonymous life to established society. I often see them hanging around Les Halles, particularly after noon, when business ends. They scavenge the remnants of fruits, vegetables, cheeses, bread—leavings that are not appetizing to look at but I suppose are edible. They pick the grounds clean like poor hungry animals."

We find one *clocharde* sunning herself on the quai, her face a mesh of broken lines, hair tinted the color of dried blood, patches of rouge on her cheeks, scruffy clothes shed on the paving stones around her. "Poor thing," Madame says. She approaches the crone. "I have something for you," and hands her a pair of shoes and heavy socks. The woman does not move. She seems about to molt into something, hopefully a different incarnation altogether. Madame adds the shoes and socks, plus a wool hat, to the pile beside the woman and we leave. "In some ways these creatures are shy," she says, as though she were referring to a doe or a squirrel.

We follow the quai westward; the sun reflects off the river in sparkling mirrors of light. Green shoots are emerging on the elms along the banks and catkins hang like ornaments on the poplars. Women dressed in pastel colors push children in baby carriages; couples stroll hand in hand. Everyone seems weightless, about to float off into the sky like helium-filled balloons. The air has the sweet odor of spring. Madame takes my arm. We find another *clocharde*, a surprisingly young woman, washing clothes on the river bank. Her arms are wet, impossibly thin, and glisten in the sun like aluminum rods. Madame hands her a sweater and a matching hat. The woman eyes us and the clothing, then her mouth twitches like a rabbit and she takes the stuff without a word; she appears wounded in some obscure way. We move on. Further down the quai there is a seated twisted figure who looks as though she could use some of Vernon's cortisone; her complexion shades toward violet and her lips are grape-colored. She rises to greet us; the newspaper she was sitting on carries the headline "Truman Sacks MacArthur." She grasps with a spidery hand the blue sweater Mme Colmar holds out to her then bows a creaky bow. "A thousand thanks, *chère Madame*," she says, her voice quavery, "you are most kind and generous." She holds up a finger as though about to say more but says nothing, the curved finger hangs in the air like the beak of a bird.

The bookseller stalls are now open along the quais, the books are bound in cracked leather—some are skinny brown-covered things stacked together so they look like upright cigars, others are more substantial, their titles embossed in gold but partially effaced, like Mme Colmar's collected volumes of de Sévigné's letters—and cover everything from the history of France to communication with the beyond. People browse but the *bouquinistes* don't actively sell, rather they sit on cloth chairs and gaze at the traffic or read, and their stalls strike me more as part of the scenery than serious businesses.

Fishermen are along the banks of the Seine, their lines in the shimmering water; Madame is buoyant as our load lightens. She waves an arm toward the far bank of the river and lightheartedly observes that the Quai des Orfèvres is ugly and the Palais de Justice pretentious. I find it impossible to believe that she is preparing for her death within three weeks. "Are you certain you won't regret this?" I ask.

"Regret what?"

"Giving away these things. Frankly speaking, I would say you have at least twenty more years of life. Why are you so insistent on making your life exactly parallel that of Mme de Sévigné?"

"But it is not I who wish our lives to parallel. It is destiny that has ordained it, not I."

"How can a sophisticated woman like you believe such nonsense?" I say with irritation. "No one knows what destiny has in store."

She squeezes my arm. "Ah, François, you suffer from the brilliance of the young. It is a marvelous malady." We reach the Pont des Arts and as though by some unspoken agreement both turn together onto the bridge; we lean on the railing, looking westward, downriver. The white stone of the Pont du Carrousel is before us, luminous in the brilliant light, and we can make out the golden horses atop their stone pylons on the Pont Alexandre III and beyond the sky reflecting blue-grey off the glass roof of the Grand Palais and further still the domes and spires of the churches, all white and cleansed and innocent in the sun. We place our arms around each other's waist. The river flows blue-green below us; a black barge glides downstream toward the Tuileries leaving eddies in the water; on the near bank a man dressed in work clothes is clipping a black poodle; the hairs slowly disperse in the breeze, disappearing among the cobblestones. The whole world appears slowed, drifting leisurely through time. "You will not die," I say to Madame.

She turns toward me and I can see her eyes blurring. "You are a fine man, François," she says and looks away.

Madame finds another woman, concave chest, moth-colored skin and of indeterminate age; hands clasped as though in prayer, the woman has a saintly appearance, as though beatified by misfortune. Madame lays the rest of the clothes beside her.

I wonder about superstition; baseball players are superstitious—Joe DiMaggio during his 56-game hitting streak made it a point to eat the identical breakfast of bacon, eggs, and grapefruit every day; Ted Williams always touches two bases coming in from the outfield; Babe Ruth used to pick up hairpins, claiming that whenever he found one he hit a home run. I've heard of poker players who think walking around the table before a game brings good luck. Irene once told me that my untied shoelace was bad luck. I suppose it's easy to transfer power to an object or become obsessed with a pattern of behavior. Maybe deep inside everyone feels a lack of control of his life, a need for some ritual to get on the good side of destiny.

I decide to visit Mme Colmar's friend, Mme Parlanges, to see if she is aware of what is happening and can bring Madame to her senses. "I am pleased to see you again," she says as she breaks out the Dubonnet and settles back in her throne-chair. The massive couches, cabinets and tables surround the heavy woman as though part of a family portrait. Mme Parlanges's face takes on the steady look it had on the day I underwent the third degree and makes me hesitant. "*Alors, jeune homme...*" she adds encouragingly.

I finally explain what Madame is doing, based on some perceived parallel between her life and that of a woman who lived three hundred years ago, and the reading of a deck of cards. "Surely this is insane," I conclude, "but I'm powerless to stop her from giving away her belongings."

Mme Parlanges squints at me during my recital, then her face smooths, apparently satisfied. "You are a noble young man. Naive, but well-intentioned. There are connections in this world that you fail to see. An earthquake in Argentina and the fall of the Pleven government are not unrelated events. Nor is the death by famine of a million souls in India unrelated to a transportation strike in France. All of human activity is part of a single vast drama. All things fit together. Mme Colmar has spoken to me many times of her life coinciding with that of Mme de Sévigné. Who are we to say that this is not so?"

I shake my head. "It's mostly the cards that have convinced her."

"There is a framework of connections," Mme Parlanges persists. "Perhaps God created all past and all future in a single blinding vision and we, through some artifice such as the tarot, can discern, however dimly and unevenly but discern all the same, how His drama will play itself out."

I can tell that the conversation is hopeless. In frustration, I say, "Don't you see, Madame, all this belief in cards, in a future written and unchangeable, removes responsibility. There's no point struggling against destiny."

"On the contrary," Mme Parlanges says. "It is struggle that determines destiny. Life is ordered imperfectly, unjustly, and all of us struggle against this arrangement. Man is not helpless. His destiny presupposes struggle."

I give up, can't handle the screwball logic. These women have known each other since they were girls, respect each other's idiosyncrasies, reason in the same bizarre way, and believe in the same mysterious connections. I suppose that's why their friendship has endured for so many years. It was hopeless.

When I leave Mme Parlanges, I begin to wonder whether I have not asked the wrong friend for help. After all, Mme Parlanges's mind is stocked with foreboding and perceives disaster in every unlit corner. When I return to the apartment, I poke around Madame's desk and find the phone number of Mme de Hauteville. I introduce myself on the telephone. Mme Colmar has indeed spoken of me and Mme de Hauteville would be delighted to receive me.

Her apartment, draperies drawn though it is mid-afternoon, is lit by pink and orange lamps and looks like an antique dealer's showroom, the furniture all rounded surfaces, adorned with ormolu and porcelain plaques and lacquered in green vernis, the chairs upholstered in damask and brocade. Mme de Hauteville resembles Mme Colmar, though taller, more substantial; her movements are rapid, competent, as she offers me tea and cheese sandwiches on minute squares of white bread. She then seats herself opposite me, on a chair with delicate rounded legs and covered in blue and gold, and leans back. I hesitate: Mme de Hauteville has taken on some of the luster of the room around her, become a part of the legend of her furnishings, and this gives her a glamour that mixes confusedly in my mind with the splendid interiors of Versailles and the distant thunder of cannon and the pursuit of empire. Her face is medal-like, an image from a gold coin.

I take a deep breath and once again explain Mme Colmar's irrational belief and behavior. Mme de Hauteville turns her head slightly to the side as I speak, as though one eye observed more acutely, more profoundly, than the other. "What is it that you expect of me?" Mme de Hauteville asks.

"That you do what I cannot. Persuade her to stop giving away her possessions, to stop believing that she will be dead in two weeks."

"But we are not discussing algebra, *Monsieur Rébair*," she says, arching a pair of expressive eyebrows. "These are not mathematical proofs to be shown correct or incorrect. These are beliefs arising from one's soul. They obey their own laws and cannot be expelled by external logic. If they are wrong then time will demonstrate this."

"But by then she will have given away all she owns," I

say in frustration, "and based only on a possible occurrence that defies belief."

Mme de Hauteville shakes her head. "The world is full of strange occurrences that defy logic. Aeschylus was killed by a tortoise dropped on his head by an eagle; Frederick the Great was saved from death by a spider that fell from the ceiling into a cup of poisoned chocolate that he was about to drink; and St. Denis, the patron saint of France, after being beheaded, carried his head in his hands for three kilometers to the spot where his cathedral now stands."

I can see that in the seventeenth century mind of Mme de Hauteville no sharp line separates legend from life. I consider giving her a brief lecture on the difference between the probable and the possible but decide against it. "And speaking of belief," she continues, "do not forget that both Cassandra and Helenus, who foretold the future with perfect accuracy, were not believed. Time alone is the final arbiter." She settles in her gilded armchair and contemplates me. "Mme Colmar cares a great deal for you. It is most satisfying to see that you reciprocate the feeling. She is a remarkable woman. She knows herself. Comfort her, remain close to her. Providence will take care of everything else."

When Mme de Hauteville shows me out, her door squeaks and an instant later I hear the wail of an ambulance. The two sounds seem mysteriously linked, as though opening the door created the ambulance. The sensation persists on the street: I pass a woman carrying a fishnet sack filled with groceries; she steps over a flyblown scrap of newspaper—the shred of paper and the housewife also seem linked, as though one could not exist without the presence of the other—and at that moment the whole city, indeed the world, seems connected as one coherent whole, in the words of Mme Parlanges, "part of a single vast drama." I wonder whether the goofy philosophy of these foreign women isn't contagious, like some wierd medieval disease, and whether it has infected me.

Curious now about de Sévigné herself, I return to the ancient volume that Madame recommended, blow away the dust, carefully turn the yellowed pages, and dip into the correspondence of the seventeenth century Marquise. My French is now sufficiently advanced that I can see past the archaicisms of spelling and I find, to my surprise, that Mme de Sévigné reads effortlessly. I'm thrust back into the gossip of the court of Louis XIV, concerts and ballets attended, meals eaten, books read, glittering soirées, brilliant wit and elegant repartee, trips to the countryside, exchanges of confidence, arguments and reconciliations, marriages, politics, advice on child rearing, psychology—from fashion to death, from God to money, there is no subject Mme de Sévigné will not touch, all helter-skelter, tumbling over each other without transition. As I read I am indeed struck by the similarities between Mme Colmar and Mme de Sévigné. Whether reading poetry, listening to music, or at the theater, both are easily moved to tears; they both believe in fortunetelling, even blush, and their moods shift rapidly; they both believe that the heart has ascendancy over the intellect. Neither reminisce, both live for the moment, and both are curious, gay and melancholy by turns. As their similarity in temperament and outlook becomes clear to me, I begin to half-believe in Mme Colmar's imminent death.

One night, I wait until we have drunk much Cointreau then I remark to Madame that I'm following her advice and reading the letters of Mme de Sévigné. I mention this in a casual way, as she's finishing the last of the liquor in her glass, and notice that my hands have grown cold as I wait for her to respond.

"Good!" she says. "That's the proper thing for you to

do." Then she throws up her hands. "Ah, how terribly forgetful of me. I must be entering the springtime of my senility. I once promised to show you the letters I possess, didn't I? Are you still interested?"

My hands are colder yet. "Yes, if it does not inconvenience you," I say, trying to keep my voice nonchalant.

"First a kiss," she says, and I taste her tongue sweet with the orange flavor of Cointreau. She goes to the rolltop desk (I can't believe the letters are in her desk!) and extracts two keys from a drawer, one small the other large, both complicated and ancient-looking, then takes me to her bedroom and switches on the overhead light. It's the first time I have ever been there. The bed is unmade and there's a stale slept-in odor mixed with a vague smell of urine. Dark heavy furniture fills the room, thick curtains sag around the window, one side drawn the other open. The bed, a heavy affair with a huge dark-wood headboard, has a thick comforter crumpled on what looks like a lumpy mattress, and fills much of the room. There's a straight-backed chair in a corner and a massive armoire against one wall. She asks me to displace the armoire; it's incredibly heavy but I manage to nudge it by degrees away from the wall. A round metal plate, which I gather is the door to a safe, protrudes from the plaster behind the armoire. The large key opens the metal door. Mme Colmar rummages among papers inside—"Useless trash," she says. "The detritus of a life."—and extracts a metal container, tarnished to a dusky gold and probably brass, about the size of a cigar box; the lid, hinged along its entire length, has a fleur-de-lis engraved into the metal. The box itself looks like a relic. Madame opens it with the small key; I expected an odor, like that which might emerge from a freshly breached tomb, but there is nothing. Greedily I peer inside.

Papers, grey-brown in color, the edges feathered like parchment, cracked in places, fit perfectly in the box. The top sheet must at one time have been folded in quarters because two creases, one vertical the other horizontal, form a cross in the center of the paper. The writing, in black ink, is surprisingly large, the letters rounded and looped, free-flowing, uniform. I cannot keep myself from reaching in but Madame yanks the box away. "The letters cannot be touched," she says. "They are much too fragile. The oil from your fingers would damage the paper." We both stare into the container; we're close. "You may hold the box if you wish," she says, reverence in her voice. I grasp the metal: it's cold and heavy, an ingot of ancient bullion from the vaults of the Sun King, transferred from hand to hand across three centuries, now miraculously in my hand. To my surprise, Madame starts to caress my body. "I have never shown these to anyone," she says. She seems sexually excited by the presence of the open box of letters. She takes the box from me and places it open upon the nightstand close to her bed then pulls me toward her. The mattress is indeed lumpy. After our lovemaking she locks the box and safe and I, with some difficulty, replace the armoire.

"Well," Lea says across her *café filtre*, "are there really any letters?" I know the right answer is to say no, to quash this thing right here, at the Café St. Claude, sitting outdoors on the Boulevard St. Germain, in the cool spring night, as the crowds and traffic hurry by. I avoid her gaze, stare at the church of St. Germain des Prés across the street, the walls dark grey, the belfry a slim black triangle against the night sky. But there is something pulling me, dragging me inexorably inward, as though the letters were a massive object whose gravitational attraction was irresistible. Madame would say I'm in the grip of destiny, that the tarot with its Fool and Knights and swords and cups and whatever else, would predict my behavior with absolute certainty, for the future is no longer under my control.

"Yes, I've seen the letters," I say, continuing to avoid Lea's eyes.

"Where are they?"

"Locked in a safe in Mme Colmar's bedroom."

"What do they look like?"

"A lot of old paper with loopy writing on it. I thought I was staring at the Dead Sea Scrolls."

"They'll just rot," Lea says in an assured voice. "Your landlady will die and leave them to her daughter." I refrain from mentioning that if you believe Mme Colmar, she'll be dead in two weeks. "You said the daughter has no children, so what she'll do is sell the letters, or give them to some archive or museum, and that'll be the end of them." She stares at me. "Do you have any idea what those letters can mean to us?"

"I can't get them," I say in a tone meant to cut off all further discussion, trying to stop her from saying what I know will come next. And indeed at that moment I knew that I could never bring myself to steal the letters.

Lea lets the subject drop, but returns to it the following day and the day after that. We're together more than ever before, as though we were chained to each other. I cannot keep from seeing her. She dresses before me, rolls on her stockings, bends to adjust the straps on her shoes, all the while she keeps up a steady drumbeat about the letters. When I try to grab her she shoves me away. Never has she seemed so desirable. "Is sex contingent on the letters?" I ask, my voice deepened, hoarse.

"Stop acting like a panting dog," Lea says. "I'm not a prostitute. I can't make love on demand. It's something I have to feel."

"Is that the answer to my question?"

Lea raises a shoulder. "It's the best you're going to get."

There is an arrogance about Lea that I now realize has always irritated me. "Look," I finally say, trying to keep my voice steady, "if screwing and the letters are tied together, then forget it. You and I are never going to screw again." I head for the door. "Fuck you," I say over my shoulder.

"You're an idiot!" she shouts after me. "Screwing me isn't the point. It's not the point at all. Ask yourself what you're really hungry for. Is it to go where you want? Do what you want? Not have to listen to anybody? Not take orders from anybody? *That's* the point! *That's* what the letters will buy for you. Think about it, goddamn it! Just think about it."

I try to bury myself in work but the letters interpose themselves. I stare into the golden box that Mme Colmar holds open before me: the writing is absolutely horizontal, disciplined, though the paper is unlined. You can tell where de Sévigné dipped her pen because there is a tiny splotch of ink and the characters formed at that point are heavier. In a circle the size of a thumbprint at the bottom of the page, the writing is faded as though a drop of liquid had fallen there.

I dream of the letters, my head entering the safe and emerging with the metal box between my teeth. I raise the lid: the words on the page incandesce, increasing in brilliance until—as though the sun itself were shining through them—I'm blinded by the radiance and must turn away, their fire remaining as a red afterglow in my head. Then I awake and stare into the darkness of my room, mouth dry, and feel myself being sucked into a maelstrom of superstition, of belief that Mme Colmar is in some way a reincarnation of Mme de Sévigné and will soon be dead.

13

April 1.

I have shown François the letters. The moment had the most profound effect on me. It was the first time in years I had cast my eyes on them and at that instant I experienced a revelation. The idea sprang to my mind, playing itself out before my eyes as it did the night I lay beside François, and I knew, knew completely and absolutely, that it was right. I had told myself that I would resolve the fate of the letters by logic alone, but the episode was so extraordinary that it had the impact of revealed truth. How could I ignore this, I who have always lived by intuition? The event stimulated my entire being and could only be consummated in one way. The letters beside me, François deep within me... it was the most satisfying sexual experience of my life. For a long moment death itself disappeared.

Madame continues to give away her clothing as well as

her books, kitchen utensils, dishes, pots and pans, lamps—if it can be placed in a shopping bag, she carries it out the door—and strips the house bare.

"With that money," Lea argues, "you don't ever have to go back to engineering. You can stay in Paris as long as you like, write as many books as you want. Winter in Cannes or Nice, even buy an apartment in Neuilly. And stop wearing drip-dry clothes." She seems to surround me, give me no respite. Why don't I just get rid of her, put her behind me, say fuck off and be gone? But something in me seeks her out, listens, can't keep from listening. "Your GI Bill money will be gone soon enough. Then what? Those letters can change your life. I just can't understand why you hesitate." She stares at me in exasperation, then her face relaxes and she moves close. Her mouth is slightly open, a beckoning cave of darkness. "Look," she says, "*you* needn't take the letters. Just let me into the apartment and get the keys for me. I'll do the rest."

I can't pinpoint the exact moment when my resolve weakened, but I think it's when I looked around the barren house and came to believe, to truly believe, that in nine days Mme Colmar would will herself to die. If that were true, then the time to take the letters was now, before Berthe Colmar took everything. I told myself, then told myself again, that Mme Colmar's sentimental attachment would soon be over; as for the daughter, her claim to the letters was merely an accident of birth and mattered less than my financial need. Lea was right—the letters would change my life. Her reasoning, like her critiquing of my stories in Boston, was hardheaded truth, unassailable. Yes the letters would change my life. I had known it all along, wanted all along to possess the letters, but lacked the courage to acknowledge it. How ridiculous it was to hesitate! Madame's Providence was shouting to me, offering me this gift with outstretched hands, yet I hesitated. For some unfathomable reason I had been chosen by fate and stupidly, obtusely, held back by a morality that mattered less with each passing moment and in nine days would matter not at all, I hesitated. How ridiculous!

And so at last I crawled into Lea's bed. But I experienced no joy in it, and when I left I was not sure whether I had won or lost.

Madame has disappeared to give away the last of her clothes—she's down to whimsical things with feathers and ruffles in shades of violet—when I let Lea into the apartment. I have trouble with the sliding cover of the rolltop desk because my hands are unsteady. I find the keys and this time have no difficulty moving the armoire. I fumble with the key in the safe and finally manage to open it. I withdraw the metal box—light from the window reflects dully off the cover, emphasizing the fleur-de-lis engraving—and extend it toward Lea. My hands are ice cold.

"The key," Lea says, her voice all business. I stare at her, empty-headed. "The key to the box!" I hand her the key; she opens the lid and we both stare at the contents. For me they are now mixed with the sweet orange taste of Cointreau and sex with Mme Colmar. Old man Colmar in his bathrobe appears in the doorway and my heart gives a mighty beat; Lea, after a glance, ignores him. She snaps the box shut, returns the key to me and heads for the door.

"Shouldn't you keep the letters and put the box back?" I ask.

"Come to my place tomorrow," she says and slips past M. Colmar and is gone. I shut the door to the safe; it closes with a decisive clang and I have the feeling that a gate has irrevocably slammed shut, isolating me forever behind a wall of misfortune. I shove the armoire back into place and turn to go. M. Colmar still stands in the doorway. For a moment, time settling with the slow regularity of sand in an hour-glass, we stare at each other across the divide of the

great matrimonial bed. I have the impression that there is
a brief flicker at the edge of his mind, then it's gone. His
eyes, in dark hollows like those of his wife, have the fixity
of an owl, hard, empty of expression. I too squeeze past him
and leave the Colmar bedroom. At that moment all my self-
justification vanished and as I fled into the street, the echo
of the clanging door still reverberating in my head, I knew
that I had done a terrible thing.

*April 10. It is strange and most frustrating but I awoke
this morning once again uncertain as to my decision. Why
is this? It is not like me to vacillate over a decision already
taken. It must be the enormity of the choice, the weight of
three-hundred years of family and precedent on my shoulders. Very well then, if logic does not work—and thus far
it has only led me to confusion—then I shall do what I
believe. I will use a tarot reading to settle this matter
forever.*

"The man to see is a certain Jacques Vadier," Lea says.
"He's a *receleur*... What do you call these people in
English? A fence."

"Mind if I come along?" I ask.

Lea doesn't seem too happy about this, but we go
together to meet with Jacques; the letters are in Lea's
briefcase, which she carries clutched against her chest as
though it were an infant. I expected Jacques to have slicked-
back hair, a Gauloise hanging from his lips, and a line of
Rolex knock-offs from his wrist to his elbow. Instead,
Jacques owns a rare books and manuscripts shop on the
Rue de Condé, a small round man with wispy white hair
who peers at us over half-moon glasses. The place smells of
dust and crumbling paper; Jacques looks as old as the
books.

"May I see the letters?" Jacques asks after Lea explains

what we have.

Lea takes the metal box from her briefcase, the lid now held shut by two heavy elastic bands. Jacques peers into the box but does not touch the letters; he raises his head, expression unchanged, and asks us to follow him as he shuffles to a table in the dusty interior of the store. He adjusts a lamp that shines deep violet light directly above the letters. The paper under the lamp is black but the writing glows with a mysterious phosphorescence. The words seem to take on a religious significance, as though we're staring at the original manuscript of the bible. Jacques snaps off the light and looks up; he doesn't appear to have undergone a religious experience, in fact his expression has never changed. He peers at us over his glasses, an ancient cherub. "At first glance they appear authentic," he says, "but to be certain I must take a sliver of the paper and subject it to chemical analysis."

Lea retrieves the box; Jacques's bent figure leads us to a beat-up wooden desk covered by a splotched blotter; three sharpened black pencils, like exclamation points, are aligned neatly to Jacques's right, and a black marble rectangle containing an inkwell and two pens in grooves lies above the pencils. We sit on straight-backed chairs in front of the desk. I admire Lea's style as she opens the box and gives it a slight shove toward Jacques. "How much are they worth?" she asks.

"It depends," Jacques says over his glasses, paying no attention to the box. "To obtain their full value you need two things, confirmation of authenticity and proof of ownership."

"You will have to make do without proof of ownership," Lea says in a peremptory manner.

"That greatly reduces their value," Jacques says.

"Reduces it to what?" she asks.

Jacques gives a French shrug. "Several hundred dollars

for the lot," he says, using what must be the universal medium of exchange in his business.

"That's ridiculous!" Lea exclaims. "Besides, if we had proof of ownership we wouldn't be here. We would go to one of the large auction houses."

"What are they worth *with* proof of ownership?" I ask, trying like a good engineer to bound the problem.

Jacques peers at me over his glasses as though I'm a rare manuscript; it must be my accent. He shrugs again. "Difficult to say. Depends on the availability of a buyer. But I would estimate a thousand, at the very most two thousand dollars in total."

Lea bangs the box shut, replaces the elastics and restores the box to her briefcase. *"Bonjour Monsieur Vadier,"* she says as she heads for the door.

"Bonjour 'sieur 'dame," Jacques says amiably.

"What now?" I ask when we're on the street.

"I'll look for another fence," Lea says. She seems a lot less sure of herself than when the letters were all theory.

"I shall be gone in five days," Madame says to me the following morning, "but before disappearing I would like to ask a favor of you."

"Anything."

"I would like a divining of your future."

"But I don't believe in any of that."

"It is not for you, dear François, but for me. Come. Indulge an eccentric old woman. We shall do it this afternoon."

Madame takes me to an apartment building in the Rue des Canettes, across the street from a restaurant of the 350 francs per porkchop variety, gives a nod of recognition as she passes the concierge, and knocks at the apartment on the ground floor. The hallway smells of damp and I can hear a child crying behind the door. There is no placard or sign of any kind. The woman that opens is surprisingly young and looks familiar. She shifts the child—who I would guess is a year old and whose face is tear-streaked— to her left arm, and shakes hands with Mme Colmar. Madame explains that she would like a reading for me while she observes. "That is unusual," the young woman says, "but I see no reason why not. First let me see if I can convince Pierrot here to take his nap." Her voice is resonant and carries a certain confidence and power. She leads us to a small round table in the dining room, in the corner farthest from the window, pulls over a chair for Madame, then disappears; the light from the window is flat, silvery. The furniture is not unlike that of Mme Parlanges, dark in color, heavy, old, I would guess inherited. A glass-covered cabinet filled with small objects, some in crystal others in porcelain, laid out as orderly as handwriting on a page, is fastened to a wall. Madame and I sit perpendicular to each other on wooden chairs with armrests; I notice my armrests are shiny, slippery; the table is chipped and stained in places; the room smells airless, dusty. I'm uneasy. Madame must sense this because she smiles at me, a smile of encouragement.

A box in dark wood, somewhat larger than a cigarette pack, lies in the center of the table; it too is chipped and stained. "Those are the cards," Madame says, gesturing with her head toward the box. Her voice carries an under-tone of awe, as though the future of the world has been trapped within the box.

The young woman strides into the room, suddenly professional, and sits at the empty place opposite me. There is a strength and energy about her that engages my atten-tion. "What is your name?" she asks.

"François," I reply.

She removes a pack of worn oversized cards from the box and hands it to me. "Shuffle," she says. I do this as best

I can. "Shuffle again." She has me repeat this six times
before she is satisfied. "Now cut the cards into three decks
using your left hand." After I have done this she turns to
Madame. "If you wish, Mme Colmar, you may choose."
Madame hesitates a moment, her left hand hovering over
the three piles, then chooses the deck to my right and closest
to her. I study the young woman: her face is a perfect oval,
framed by black hair that falls in tendrils on her forehead
and around her face, her eyes are far apart, slightly oriental,
a black dot the size of a pinhead emphasizes an exquisitely-
shaped mouth. She takes the deck Madame has chosen and
looks directly at me: my heart gives a mighty thunk—she
resembles Irene.

"What is your question?" she asks me.

I stare at her: her eyes are dark, beautiful—it's Irene
come to divine my future. "He wishes to ask, What will I
make of my life?" Madame answers.

Irene lays ten cards on the table, face down, two in the
center, four around them to form a cross, and four in a
vertical line to my right. I was twenty-two when Irene and
I were married, she nineteen, a butterfly who flirted with
every man who came along, even flirted on our honey-
moon. I think it was her way of testing, a constant need for
proof that she was desirable. I don't believe she had an
affair until just before we separated but that may be wishful
thinking. Clothes were important to her, the latest fashions
no matter how nutty. She went in for iridescent chambray
dresses in lilac or pistachio, huge pearl-colored buttons,
high heels with preposterous ankle straps, goofy hem-
lines—scalloped or harem style—weird belts, even had a
paprika-colored cummerbund, and one night she showed
up in a Cossack jacket as though she'd just emerged from
the steppes of central Asia. The strange thing was that she
looked great in whatever she wore. I was working and
going for a master's at night so every minute was precious

to me. But she always wanted to go out, go dancing, go to the Cape, go to Vermont or New Hampshire, *do* something. It wasn't always clear what that something was. To get out, to *go*, that was the idea. We couldn't afford a car but she bought a sputtering 1939 Mercury anyway. The car was a chronic cash drain and made me desperate. We had a tiny apartment in Somerville; her first purchase was a modernistic coffee table with elliptical holes in the legs like a Henry Moore or Jean Arp sculpture. For the first six months of our marriage it was the only furniture in the living room. Then she bought a lamp, one of those slender futuristic affairs, and a green and white stuffed chair. That's as far as the living room ever got. I remember it now with infinite tenderness.

Irene turns over the first card, one of the two at the center of the cross. It depicts a tower being struck by lightning, the top blown off and in flames; two figures leap from windows and hurtle toward rocky crags below. The background is unrelieved black. Madame stares at the card, frowns. "This card is your starting point," Irene says. "It is the now of your life. It says that you are entering a period of upheaval and violent change, a tearing down of existing structures and convictions. It is also a time of opportunity as well as a time of tension." Irene concentrates on the card, which from her perspective is inverted, as she says this, and her voice carries extraordinary conviction.

She turns over the second center card and lays it horizontally across the first. "This card represents the force that complements The Tower," she says. The image is of two youths each holding a cup. "The two of cups reveals that at this period of your life opposing forces struggle within you—heart and mind, masculine and feminine, morality and sin. No one can live this way and ultimately you will choose. The rest of the cards will reveal the choices that you shall make."

157

One Friday evening, after eighteen months of marriage, Irene didn't come home. Didn't show up the whole weekend. I thought she'd had an accident; I telephoned the local hospital, the police; I couldn't bring myself to call her parents, her friends. She phoned me at work Monday morning and said she would come by the apartment and pick up her things that afternoon. I took the rest of the day off and waited. She didn't seem surprised to see me, just packed while I watched. I thought sex might be a way to keep her from leaving but she said in a clipped matter-of-fact way that if I wanted to screw her I'd have to kill her first. Of course I should have known that things were fucked up when her vocabulary changed. She started to use words like spiritual unfoldment and dynamic joy and transcendental reality and union with the absolute. I ignored all that until she got stuck on the word "infinite": infinite consciousness, infinite light, infinite union, even once called herself daughter of the infinite. I asked her what this infinite shit was all about. She said my problem was that I had lousy karma and that was screwing up my life and would always screw up my life, and she didn't want any part of it.

Irene turns over the third card, the top arm of the cross and the one directly above the crossed pair in the center. The card is upside down to me. "You may turn the card around to view it better," she says, "but then return it to its former position." A man on crutches and a destitute woman trudge through the snow; above them is a brightly lit window decorated with five pentacles. I return the card as she says, "This is the first indication of choice. The pentacles refer to a preference for the material elements of life, but it is the inversion that is troublesome. It betokens an obsessive emphasis on work to the exclusion of the other aspects of living, while the two figures foretell a blind and lonely struggle toward material goals while ignoring the world around you."

She turns over the fourth card, the one at the bottom of the cross. It too is inverted. The card depicts a chariot driven by a warrior and pulled by two lions, one black the other white, both with human faces. Quarter moons rest on each of the charioteer's shoulders, castles fill the background. "The fourth card provides a vista, a longer view of purpose. The inverted chariot and its figures indicate a life of conflict as you spur yourself toward goals that forever lie just beyond your grasp, sometimes dissipating your energies in self-indulgence and hedonism." Irene looks up and gazes at me with her magnificent eyes. "The charioteer is forever alone, and so the card also implies a lonely one-sided life."

Irene told me while she packed that she had taken up with an Indian, a swami, a man who had achieved mastery over his body. She said that among his accomplishments he could drink something and pee it out only a minute later. I said I didn't think that was such a big deal because I could do the same thing with beer. He was a strict vegetarian and had convinced Irene to be the same. They sat around and ate cauliflower and broccoli together while he explained all about the Bhagavad-Gita and the Upanishads and Vishnu and Siva, and all that Hindu malarkey. The Indian, whose name was Chandak, said he could make his heart stop and demonstrated for her. Irene stopped packing when she recounted this: she had held her fingers against his wrist while he squeezed his eyes shut and concentrated—his lips turned blue and she swore his pulse stopped. What impressed hell out of me was not the heart business at all but that he could hold an erection for hours. Irene told me this in passing, as she stuffed a last skirt into the loaded suitcase; she might as well have been commenting on the weather. When Irene snapped the third valise shut, she asked me to carry out her three cases as though I were a bellboy at a hotel. When I finished loading them into the trunk of the Mercury I thought she was going to give me a tip. Then she looked at me squarely for the first time and said, "Well good-bye, Franklin. I'm sorry it didn't work out." I thought I detected a glimmer of tenderness as she said this but maybe it was only because I wanted it so badly. Then she drove off. She never looked back and she never waved and I watched until the car disappeared.

Irene turns over the fifth card, the left arm of the cross. "This card reflects your endowment, the strength and skill you bring to your life." The card is titled The Magician. A young man in a red robe holds a wand in the air, an infinity sign sits like a halo above his head. "Notice the table before him," she says. "Lying on it is a cup, a pentacle and a sword; these, together with the wand in his hand, make up all the symbolic tools of the tarot. The card foretells competence and skill in your endeavors. The sign above his head indicates a long life. Also notice the serpent around his waist, stating that you shall always be surrounded by temptation." She shakes her head, frowns and looks up. "The magician achieves his effects through artifice and illusion and so you shall forever doubt whether your attainments are real or only an illusion and at bottom a sham."

I glance at Madame: she raises her head from the cards. There is pity in her face and the look she has before we embrace. The whole affair seems to be getting out of hand and I would like to leave when Irene says, "The next is the card of destiny," and turns over the card at the right arm of the cross. It too is inverted. Irene nods that I may reverse the card to study it: a crowned king in a red cape holds a sword in his hand and sits on a throne. "This is the King of Swords," she says. "In maturity, then, you shall have power and authority. But the king is inverted: a just man, he is nevertheless somber, alone, and no great pleasure comes to him from the exercise of his sovereignty."

I met Chandak when Irene and I convened at the lawyer's to sign the divorce papers. Irene wore a sari. I expected Chandak to look like Nehru, but he was a squat ugly little guy with black inky eyes, shorter than Irene. Very courteous. I never really looked at the papers; all I could think of was this son of a bitch forcing Irene into those acrobatic positions you see in the Kamasutra, or whatever they call those pornographic Indian books, and keeping her at it for hours. I don't know if they ever married or not, but somehow I doubt it.

The next card, the bottom one in the ladder of four cards to my right, is the Knight of Wands: a youth in armor on a charging red horse carries a flowering wand. I catch the word honor but don't follow Irene's explanation; I'm still back there out of my head over the ravishing of my wife by Chandak.

"This card asks the real question," Irene says, her hand above the second card from the bottom. I try to concentrate. The delicate veins on her hand seem themselves to carry an important message. She turns over the card and it too is inverted. An old man dressed in a grey cloak holds aloft a lantern with one hand and supports himself on a yellow staff with the other. He's alone on a barren field of snow. "He is The Hermit," Irene says, "and he seeks an answer to the question How shall I find happiness? The inversion foresees that you shall never find it—rather you shall lead a long life, much of it in isolation and abandonment, and happiness shall forever elude you." Madame I now notice has tears in her eyes. Fortunately there are only two cards to go.

The ninth card, I'm relieved to see, depicts three happy young women, one wears a red cape and each holds a yellow cup in the air. "You shall have at least three children, most of whom shall be female. But notice that on no other card does a woman appear. That is most unusual. Your wife, and women generally, shall play little part in your life."

Irene looks at me. "And now we come to the last card," she says, "the card of summary." She turns over the card and I hear Madame draw in her breath. A young man, dressed in a gay costume, a stick with a sack at its end slung over his shoulder, a white rose in his hand, head high, approaches the edge of a cliff; a dog barks at his feet. I recognize the card from the description Madame gave me of the tarot reading that preceded the death of Laurent. It is The Fool. Irene sighs. "You shall forever be a mixture of innocence and wisdom," she says. "Heedlessness and risk shall always be a part of your life, and when you cause unhappiness in others rarely will you be aware of it."

Irene gazes at the cards, now all face up. "There are five trump cards," she says. "Usually there are no more than two or three. With this many trumps predictions are very reliable. The many inverted cards divine the persistence of turmoil in your life." She further scans the spread of cards. "Observe the colors. There is a preponderance of reds and yellows, colors of agitation, and a lack of blue, the color of tranquility."

Irene stares at me. There is pity in her lovely face, her splendid eyes. She really believes. This tale of my life that she has invented like improvised theater from these little pasteboard pictures, she truly believes. "I had expected The Devil and possibly The Hanged Man," she says, "but neither came."

"Is that good?" I ask.

"Yes," she says and at that moment, as I stare into Irene's beautiful face, I know that I love her and that it will take forever to get over it.

When we leave I hear Pierrot crying and Irene hurries away.

"It is not what I expected," Madame says. "You have a difficult road before you, François, touched by life in your way the same as the rest of us have been touched in ours." We pass the Mabillon entrance to the metro, in the Place d'Acadie, and as the subway odor strikes our nostrils Madame takes my arm as though to protect me. "The most revealing card for me," she says, "was the first, The Tower, for that is where our lives, yours and mine, intersected. I could not help but feel that the two poor souls falling toward the rocks were you and I, that my fate had dragged you down as well, that Mme de Sévigné had inadvertently fastened herself onto you."

But I'm not really listening. I'm back in the tiny apartment in Somerville with the crazy Henry Moore coffee table and my capricious Irene and that son of a bitch Chandak who took it all away from me and the immutable fact that I can change none of it, ever.

14

April 13.

I depended on the reading to provide some further revelation but none came. What did I expect? It was foolish of me to think the cards would say, "Yes, this idea is good." That is really asking too much. François shall have a difficult life... we need no tarot to divine this for anyone born. What matters is that he shall be honorable, successful, and have daughters. Very well then. The time to choose is now and I have chosen. I shall see Maître Denoix this afternoon and have him draw up the papers. He will think me insane...

The night before the anniversary of Mme de Sévigné's death, Mme Colmar and I lie in my bed together. She has placed an oversized envelope on the nightstand. "I understand you have spoken with my friends," she says. "That was most considerate of you. To concern yourself so over my welfare. But it will change nothing."

"Why do you say that?"

"There is a complicated answer and a simple one. The simple answer is that Mme Parlanges believes in connections, and the more fanciful the more believable, and as for Mme de Hauteville, she maintains that life is stranger than we know, stranger even than we can imagine. So you see my link to Mme de Sévigné satisfies them both."

"And the church?" I ask. "What would be their view of this affair?"

Madame gives a dismissive grunt. "The church is now populated by administrators, *fonctionnaires*, harried men running a large and complex enterprise. Most priests are comfortably settled in dogma and the original vision on which Peter built the church is misty for most, nonexistent for many." She is quiet for a moment. "But for a few the vision has remained... Interesting that you mention the church. I knew an old priest, a man of great piety. I had not seen him for years and thought him dead. But something told me to look for him anyway and I found him, an ancient Saint Francis, doddering among the votive candles, but alive. This was yesterday morning. I asked him to hear my confession... It was a beautiful confession that lasted three hours." I can't imagine what Madame could possibly confess that would last more than ten minutes.

"After tomorrow I shall be gone," Mme Colmar says, her voice serious. I imagine her, in the deep center of her being, like some emaciated holy man beside the Ganges dressed in a loincloth and seated cross-legged upon a rock, willing herself to die. "I have thought deeply about my affairs," she continues, "and have decided to give you an important gift. Something that means a great deal to me." She pauses a moment, lets the weight of silence accumulate, and I sense that she is about to say something of great consequence. Then, in a slow measured voice, she says, "I will give you the Sévigné letters."

"What? Oh, no!" I exclaim. "You can't do that! I will not accept them."

"Ah, you're a sweet young man, François," she says, kissing me. "It's altogether proper for you to object. But after my death the letters will go to my daughter." Then to my astonishment she spells out the ultimate fate of the letters in the identical scenario given me by Lea. "Berthe will only sell the letters or donate them to some museum. I don't need her for this. *I* can give the letters to a museum. They will then lie there, naked, forever exposed to the peeping eyes of strangers. I cannot bring myself to do this."

"I have had prepared a document in two copies," Madame continues, "saying that being of sound mind, I hereby give of my own free will the Mme de Sévigné letters to M. Franklin *Rébair*, and have had this document witnessed by an attorney. I have even been careful to spell your name correctly. I suppose I could have left you the letters in my will, but I fear the testament might be annulled by my daughter because of the years the letters have belonged to my family, or she might contend that I was insane when I amended the will. In this way I can circumvent all that and you can take the letters immediately after my death, before my will is read."

She takes the envelope from the nightstand. "This is proof that you own the Sévigné letters," she says as she removes a document from the envelope and hands it to me. It consists of heavy, ivory-colored paper, half-covered with typing, four stamps along the top and a red seal near the bottom. For the first time I see that Mme Colmar's given name is Honorine, and this small revelation causes an inordinate wave of tenderness to pass through me. I pronounce her name aloud and kiss her. "*Chéri*," she says, and touches my face. "My mother, I was told, was a great admirer of Balzac. She was convinced the child she was carrying was a boy and planned to name him Honoré, after

Balzac. When I came along she settled for Honorine. I couldn't stand the name as a child. Later I grew resigned to it but have never liked it." She closes her thumb and forefinger on the edge of the document and for a moment both our hands grasp the paper. "There is another copy of this that has remained with the lawyer... You know where the letters are, you know where the keys are..."

Madame hesitates then lets go of the document. I fold it and replace it in the envelope. Madame hesitates a moment longer; I can feel her preparing something important. "There is, however, one thing I would ask of you, François." She waits to be sure she has my complete attention. "I ask for your solemn promise that you will protect the letters and keep them within your own family. One day you will marry and have daughters. I ask that you pass the letters on to your first daughter and she to hers and thereby establish a new line for the letters. They shall become the valuable objects of your family as they have been of mine for eight generations. In this way I may die knowing that the most precious thing I own has been provided for... Will you promise me that?"

This was clearly not the moment to raise an objection and so, unable to look at Mme Colmar, I say, "I promise to keep and protect your letters."

"Very well then, do not wait but take them immediately after I am gone... Shall we take one last look at them together?" she asks, moving toward the edge of the bed.

"If you wish," I say and grab her and hug her close and kiss her, and finally succeed in making her forget about the last look.

The following day is April 17th, the anniversary of Mme de Sévigné's death.

April 16: My dearest François, I write you this, which you will read—if indeed you ever do read it—after my

167

death, as the final words of an old woman who loved you.

I have given you the possession closest to me and to my family. It was an act of intuition that sprang from the heart, with little logic, but I know that it is right. My heart and mind have not always been in agreement. I have often found it difficult to harmonize the two opposing parts of my nature; unlike Plato's charioteer, I have been unable to make the two steeds pull as one.

With you the letters will leave this exhausted old continent and start a new life in a new world. All things fit together under an all-knowing Providence. I am convinced that it was Providence that sent you to me, during these final months of my life, to provide a new beginning for the letters. I know they will bring good fortune to your daughter and to her daughters for many generations to come. I also know that you will treasure and protect them, and treat them with the same care as my ancestors have for three centuries.

For the last month I have tried to concentrate on every moment and in this way slow the passage of time. If I have seemed grasping or possessive to you, this is the reason. I am certain you will understand and forgive me. I have said good-bye to my friends, written to those far away, and even said good-bye to poor Gustave as he regarded me with his dead eyes. To Berthe, alas, there is nothing to say. Mme Parlanges will notify her of my death and I have left her a note with regard to funeral arrangements.

So, mon cher François, *you go to live your life and I to my end. Do remember, there is no hard wall that separates character from fate. No matter how unjust, imperfect, and painful your life may seem, it must always be confronted with honor and dignity. Only in this way can it be bettered or indeed lived at all. The ultimate sin, indeed the only sin, is to betray those who trust you. To do this is to betray yourself and in this way settle your destiny. But you*

François are incapable of betrayal. I see it in your eyes and in the penumbra of innocence that surrounds you. It is this knowledge that gives me the courage to face the ultimate mystery with my soul at peace, knowing that my letters— the letters of my family—are in your hands and safe forever.
With deepest and most profound affection,
Honorine Colmar

Mme Colmar does not appear nor does my morning hot water and bread, butter and jam. I'm apprehensive that she may already be dead. I poke my head into her bedroom: she's lying in bed staring at the ceiling, a book open on her chest. "Ah, François, I was expecting you. I knew you would be here. Come beside me. Share the last hours of a dying woman." She says this in a natural way, with no trace of irony. She places the book on the nightstand; it's the last volume of Mme de Sévigné's letters, those written near the end of her life. She pulls me toward her and kisses me and to my surprise does indeed seem feverish. "Lie close to me," she says. "Stay with me... I had the most horrible nightmare last night. I dreamt that all vowels had been forbidden in speech and the only sounds people made were harsh spitting guttural noises."

I hold her for a while then have to go to the bathroom. When I return Madame is again on her back, only now her eyes are closed and her hands crossed on her chest, as though she were lying in state. The skin across her cheekbones seems stretched tighter, the hollows of her eyes darker, her mouth sunk inward, corpse-like. "If you can be frank anywhere," she says, "it's on your deathbed." Her voice startles me, as though a skull had spoken. I sit on the side of her bed and she turns toward me. "Is this writing of yours a serious affair?"

"I'm not sure," I say, "but I doubt it."

"Good. I'm pleased to hear this. Do not take offense,

François, but I do not believe you have the vocation. I cannot picture you spending your life alone in a room, with ink-stained fingers, creating literature. Providence gave different talents to men just as it planted different trees in the forest. Go back to your *métier*. Go out into the world. That's where your future lies." This bit of career counseling seems to have exhausted her because she lies back and once again closes her eyes and crosses her hands on her chest.

The old man wanders in—his bathrobe, I now notice, has a torn sleeve—and stands beside the bed. "What will become of M. Colmar?" I ask.

"He will finally go to a *maison de retraite*," Madame says without opening her eyes, "where he should have gone years ago."

Suddenly Madame jumps up. "My God! I had almost forgotten! There is something I must give you. I have kept a journal for the past twelve months, to record the last year of my life. It's an oversized green-covered notebook, the kind in which Gustave wrote his equations. You will find it on my desk. Take it whenever you wish. I'm finished with it but cannot bear the thought of throwing it out. You need not read the foolishness I have written, just keep the book. In this way something of me, and something intimate, will remain with you. Perhaps on some cold winter's night, when you are discouraged, you will look at it, touch it, and remember the old woman you once knew in Paris." Madame seems doubly exhausted after this speech; she closes her eyes and drops back into her death position.

The room is absolutely still for a long while. "Please read to me," Madame says in a soft voice. "My poetry volume is in the *salon*." I poke around the living room and find the anthology on the coffee table (the grey lace doily is gone), then notice her green notebook on the desk, hesitate, then take it to my room. When I return I move the straight-backed chair close to her bed and begin the reading with de

Musset, one of her favorites, then Baudelaire—when I come to the lines "*Bientôt nous plongerons dans les froides ténèbres;/Adieu, vive clarté de nos étés trop courts,*" I look up and there are tears on her cheeks—then Mallarmé and finally Apollinaire. Part of the time I don't understand what I'm reading but try to add some expression anyway. After an hour the muscles around my mouth ache from the sustained effort of making these alien sounds. From time to time Madame absently corrects my pronunciation.

The day passes; Madame touches neither food nor water. In the evening she totters to the kitchen and prepares M. Colmar's dinner then returns to her bed and her death position. She seems somehow simplified, reduced to the essence of herself. She lies astonishingly still. I imagine her heart slowing; I'm tempted to place a mirror before her mouth to see if she's still breathing. To my surprise I now find it difficult to look at her, and when I do something nags at me, something messy that I push away. I suddenly discover that I'm starving and sneak out to a small restaurant in the *quartier* and have a 315-franc pork chop with fried potatoes. When I return nothing has changed: Madame has not moved. After a while M. Colmar wanders in, takes off his bathrobe and hangs it in the empty armoire—he's wearing longjohns, stained yellow at the crotch—and slides into bed beside Madame; she moves over; I get up to leave. "Stay François," she says. "Do not go."

"Come to my room," I say.

"No. I wish to die in my own bed." She shoves M. Colmar aside. "Here, switch off the light and lie beside me." So the three of us lie on the matrimonial bed. There is a sudden foul smell. "*Cochon!*" Madame exclaims. I gather that M. Colmar has farted. No one moves; M. Colmar starts to snore, a rhythmic purr followed by a soft whistle. "What time is it?" Madame asks.

I glance at the luminous dial of my watch. "Ten-thirty,"

I reply. Madame reassumes her death position. Despite the cramped quarters I'm starting to doze off when I hear Madame say, her voice soft, not a whisper so much as feeble, distant, as though already coming from another world, "I have tried to be ruled by my heart and not my head. This was most true in times of disaster. When Laurent drowned there was no refuge and no recourse from the anguish. I did not shrink from it but allowed it to possess me. My husband—always a classicist, a believer in order, clarity, reason—remained 'courageous' and disappeared into the misty oblivion of his equations. That moment marked the beginning of his own death. I suppose that it is the losses in my life—Laurent, my parents when I was but a child, my grandparents when I was in my adolescence, relatives and friends slain in two wars, poor Gustave—that has made anxiety a part of me, always fearful that whoever I love will be snatched from me. When friends confided their anxieties to me, I reminded them of Voltaire's comment on his deathbed, 'I have had a life filled with trouble, most of which never happened.' But I have been unable to follow my own advice."

I reply in a whisper, as though we're two doomed men reviewing our lives an hour before our execution. "But you have searched for comfort in guides to the future, looked for divinations, signs, secrets... Is it anxiety that compelled you to do this?" I ask myself why I'm interrogating a dying woman on her beliefs.

"Perhaps, but unlike my husband I long ago concluded that reality cannot be reduced to scientific formulations. Neither Mme Parlanges nor Mme de Hauteville are wrong in their belief in connections and the strangeness of life. It is these affinities that influence our future... I have tried to accept things as they are, which I suppose is the beginning of wisdom... We are not born with wisdom, you know, each of us must discover it for himself. I picture wisdom as a mountain we spend a lifetime trying to scale, to gain perspective and at last see the panorama whole. No one can do it for us—each of us climbs the mountain alone. One need not be a genius to realize that life cannot be taught, it can only be lived."

All this talk about wisdom and life has made me sleepy again. I have the feeling that here in the dark of Mme Colmar's bedroom life's deepest mysteries are being revealed, yet all I want to do is sleep. I try to embrace sleep, to sink into it, because it drives away the messiness that continues to nag at me. Mme Colmar lies still for a long while. I must have dozed off because her voice startles me. "The death of my son made me aware of my own mortality, the shortness of our days. Since then I have imagined an infinite swamp of blackness around me, always ready to swallow me and into which one day—this day—I will sink. This has never saddened me, rather it made me aware of the preciousness of each moment and how wasteful it is not to savor it completely. I have always strived to experience the moment, to feel the bone and marrow of it, not only the important occasions but also the small instants—a conversation, a concert, even reading. You know, in the everyday world one is rarely in contact with oneself. We become interchangeable with each other, as alike as cows in a meadow. I have struggled to remain myself, uniquely myself, by feeling each instant, allowing even trifles—a ripe Camembert, a good bottle of Beaujolais, the leaves in autumn—to affect me. But then small things have always mattered in France. When I read that Vatel, the Prince de Condé's maître d'hotel, killed himself because the fish for the grand dinner for Louis XIV at Chantilly had not arrived in time, it did not strike me as completely unreasonable."

I'm still back with poor defeated Vatel, putting a gun to his head over the fish, when Madame's soft voice, in the deathbed hush, begins again. "I have dipped into the existentialists, Sartre in particular, and have come away disgusted. They deny any historical sense, claim man is personally and objectively without history. What nonsense! I am not an animal. My heritage is as much a part of me as the color of my eyes. How can we endure without continuity with the past?"

I am about to say, "But Madame, the existentialists, like Freud, believe that man *wants* to live with his illusions. And you yourself often prefer superstition to logic." But decide this is not the moment for dialectic argument.

Madame seems to divine my comment. "At bottom," she says, "I prefer passion, for without it existence is a pale and dreary thing."

M. Colmar changes position and the bed squeaks, then we all shift position. "It is in love that I have been weakest," Madame says, "all my needs, fears and vulnerabilities revealing themselves despite me."

"But you give yourself so completely."

"How else is one supposed to love? I have tried, often unsuccessfully, not to allow love to decay into jealousy, and have, like Proust, been baffled at how difficult—no impossible—it is to know someone you love, the one you are closest to."

Madame's monologue now wanders, or perhaps I keep drifting in and out of sleep and only catch fragments of it; her voice is softer, more feeble yet. "I have avoided worship, praying uselessly to a closed heaven... It's a shame that I have spent my life in the city. I have always adored dark woods and country solitude, the light of autumn and the new leaves of spring... I am an evening person, *une femme du crépuscule*, when the world is seen in the gauzy half light of dusk, the unreal hour of the day. At such moments you can feel the earth turning, sense the presence of all those who have died since the beginning of time... I have watched age transform old friends into grotesques of their former selves. Two disastrous wars did not help. They created death and ruin all around us. Things are not well arranged, you know, and there is far more pain than joy."

How did I get into this mess, I ask myself. I think of the Sévigné letters, what Madame has said of my writing, and it all swirls together, one big whirling mess. As Madame continues, her voice close to my ear, I perceive, there in the darkness, as though it were a glittering murderous top that I had set spinning, that this mess is of my own creation.

And so I awaited Mme Colmar's death as an event that would absolve me of all guilt, wipe clean the theft of the letters since they would be legitimately mine. But I knew in my heart that Madame's death would make no difference, that nothing could ever set right my betrayal of her trust in me. And so I tried to sink into sleep, to escape the mess whirling about my head there in the darkness of Mme Colmar's bedroom.

"Montaigne says that we attach too little value to the things we possess," Madame goes on, "and overvalue anything strange, absent, not ours. Well, all we really possess is the present, and I have tried to live it fully and not spend time reminiscing about the past or anticipating what may happen. Those who do otherwise only find satisfaction in regret or expectation, in the unchangeable past or the shadowy future. Never do that, François. Now is the moment, the only moment that is real, truly yours... Too much thinking is not good. It will make you hesitant, even paralyzed, and suck the joy out of life."

Then in a voice I can barely make out, she says, "I have often thought of life as a farce and seen myself as a character in an endless Molière play... I think I have played my part rather well... It has all been most interesting..." Then there is only the rhythmic snoring of M. Colmar.

I'm awakened by a nudge against my shoulder. "What time is it?" Madame asks.

175

I check my watch. "It's ten minutes past midnight."

"Are you sure?"

"Positive."

"Ah," Madame says, more an expulsion of breath than a word. She turns on her side away from me and toward M. Colmar.

I get out of their bed and return to my room. Perversely, I feel disappointed, as though it were the conclusion of a scientific experiment that turned out badly.

I search for Lea first thing the following morning. She's not in her apartment and not at the Sorbonne and no one has seen her. I pace around the Rue Jacob, leave, wander the neighborhood, return, ask the concierge—a nervous, flat-chested woman always dressed in black—whether Lea is in; she gives me only the briefest of side-to-side head shakes. I hear Mme Colmar's feeble voice reflecting on a lifetime and think of the mess I have created—it has become static, like the dog shit on the sidewalk in front of Lea's apartment house that I sidestep as I pace the street scanning the passersby for Lea. I use the pissoir on the Rue de l'Université; as I leave an executive type rushes in, his pecker out while he's still on the street. People come and go in Lea's building—an old man, a silver-headed cane held forward like a weapon, a well-dressed purposeful young woman, her heels clicking on the pavement as she disappears around a corner, an ageless woman with a pale green scarf who enters and leaves three times, glancing warily at me as she passes. A mother with terrific legs hustles a kid home from school, a man in blue overalls rides by on a bicycle, a *baguette* slung like a rifle over his shoulder, street cleaners in green uniforms run water along the curbs then sweep it toward the sewers with ratty-looking brooms, the bristles a delicate chartreuse color. The vague noise of the city seems to grow louder, strident, as the day passes and mixes in my mind with the savage shouts of another era, of revolution, of moaning bodies dragged through the streets and the salt taste of blood.

The street lights have come on when Lea finally returns. "I want the Sévigné letters back," I say. "Right now. I just can't live with this. I've got to give the old lady back her letters. And do it now. Tonight. Right now." The words come cascading out as though a dam ruptured.

"Why are you suddenly having this moral crisis?"

"Look, there's no explaining these things. I've thought about it and that's what I want to do. Give me the letters." I can't bring myself to tell Lea anything else.

Lea contemplates me for a long moment. "All right," she says. "But they're not here."

"Where are they?"

"I'm not crazy enough to keep them in this apartment. They're in a safe at the Crédit Lyonnais in the Place Maubert. They open at ten."

"We'll go together."

"I have an exam in the morning. This can wait until after lunch. Come back here about two tomorrow afternoon and I'll give you the letters."

"To hell with your exam. I'll meet you at the bank at ten."

Lea's body is stiff and her eyes hard as nailheads. "I won't be at the bank at ten. Come here at two."

I study Lea's face and decide at that instant that I don't like her, in fact never liked her. "You wouldn't con me, would you?" I say. "I'm not one of your pharmacists, you know. I expect to see those letters tomorrow."

Lea's gaze never wavers. "Don't give me crap, Franklin. I said you'll have them and that's it."

15

The following morning I am at my desk, unable to concentrate, my thoughts shifting between the letters and my book. A fly buzzes around the room then thuds over and over against the windowpane; I track it down and mash it with the back of my notebook then clean the mess on the glass and on the notebook with a dirty sock. I'm depressed. Mme Colmar was right: this writing business will get me nowhere. It now seems preposterous to me that I would spend my life doing this lonely thing. At that moment I remember the subject matter of my last master's course, see it written in stark white on a blackboard: Maxwell's equations. I recall the instructor, a middle-aged German woman, a refugee we were all certain, named Cecilie Lübben (she insisted on the umlaut). When she first spoke of the great Scottish physicist she pronounced his full name, James Clerk Maxwell, deepest respect in her voice. She wrote his equations on the board with a reverent hand then commented on their elegance, their economy. Toward the end of the course I decided that Cecilie—who wore no wedding band and who we imagined a spinster—loved Maxwell, loved more than his genius, loved the physical man, and the great tragedy of her life was that she had been born seventy years too late and could not take the flesh and blood Maxwell to her breast.

I sense that this recollection of school and equations carries a message: the time may well have come to return to the U.S. and engineering, to the flickering screen of an oscilloscope, the orange glow of vacuum tubes, the odor of melting solder. I find this thought more depressing yet.

There's a peremptory knock on my door and before I can answer Mme Colmar's daughter, Berthe, is in the room, her face flushed. "I must ask you to leave," she says. "I mean today. This moment."

"What have I done?"

"Whose money do you think *maman* spends on you? Certainly not her own. As I told you when we first met—she has no money. Papa's pension barely keeps them alive. No, it is *my* money that she spends... Do you think you're unique? She has been seducing her boarders for years. She only boards young men and, in fact, they all resemble you."

I'm shaken by this revelation but come to Madame's defense anyway. "Your mother has a right to live her life any way she chooses."

"I can always tell when things reach the gigolo stage," Berthe says, paying no attention to my comment, "because *maman* insists on more money and her reasons for needing the money become more fanciful. But now she has gone further than even I thought her capable. She has emptied the house of her clothing, books, kitchen utensils, virtually everything moveable, to pay for you."

I get to my feet and am about to protest when Mme

Colmar enters the room, her eyes puffy, face grey, as though she hasn't slept in days. "I have just asked your *poule* to leave," Berthe says to her mother, her voice retaining the business-like edge she used with me. "I will pay for your food and the roof over your head, but not for your amorous adventures."

The old woman straightens, moves beside me and takes my arm. "You cannot do that," she says, her voice rich with dignity. "You cannot dictate who lives in my house."

"We have had this scene before, *maman*," Berthe says in a tired voice. "Let us not go through it again. It is very simple. Either he leaves or I cease to send you money."

"You view all this as though it were an affair of accounting," Madame says; I can feel her body tighten. "An amorous adventure you call it. You live this sterile life, buried in your dingy store, stroking little girls that you've chained to sewing machines, then you have the audacity to come here and criticize me. Who are you to dictate who stays in my house and who goes?"

The two women stare at each other. Berthe's face has turned to stone. "You choose," she finally says. "Either François or the money."

Madame suddenly kisses me on the mouth then turns back toward her daughter. "I love François!" she says melodramatically.

"*Mais voyons, maman*," Berthe says, her face weary and revolted. "You don't love François any more than I do. You're in love with love and he's just a convenient object. And all this before the eyes of Papa. It's disgusting."

"Papa is dead," Mme Colmar says. "Only he's not yet buried. My life would be far simpler if he were. Do you even remotely comprehend the burden that he is? For you everything is easy. You send me a few francs each month and wash your hands of us. But I know very well what you want, to lock me behind these four walls and make of me a walking corpse like your father."

The two women continue, the French too fast and fatiguing for me to follow, and I drift away. My depression, the confusion of my life, this mess around me, is suddenly more than I can bear. I find the bickering women sickening. But I do hear Madame say one thing, almost in a whisper, as though speaking to herself: "You cannot know what it means to once again be young." Then Berthe answers and I can stand no more of it. I feel decision—as I would feel it again in the same way at other critical times in my life, like a tumbler in a lock clicking into place—take hold. I interrupt the women. "There is no need to discuss me as though I were an object with no will of my own," I say. "I'm leaving." In my mind these women are already moving away from me, imploding into the past.

"No, no, *chéri*," Mme Colmar says, clutching me close to her body, jerking me back to the present, "you cannot go." For the first time I detect panic in Madame's voice. Berthe regards both of us; she suddenly resembles her father, eyes spent. I try to edge away from Mme Colmar. For an instant we all stare at each other: the scene is fixed and seems extraordinarily lit, as though the roof has blown away and we are all frozen in the stark glare of the sun.

Madame lets go of me and faces her daughter. "You are despicable," she spits at her. "You're small, dried up, eaten by envy. Keep your money. Choke on it. I will sell flowers on the street, anything, but you will never again dictate how I live." I wonder whether Madame hasn't lost her head, carried away by anger and rhetoric; and in fact, at that moment, eyes wide, lips drawn tight against her teeth, she appears quite insane.

Berthe turns toward the door. "Wait," Mme Colmar says in a voice that I barely recognize, "I will never accept another sou from you. You and I shall never again have anything to do with each other. And of course you shall never have the one thing of value that I possess."

Berthe Colmar turns and scrutinizes her mother, her brow pulled together. "What are you saying... Have you sold the letters?" Her eyes are now squinted and her mouth partly open.

Madame stares at her daughter. "You must have the soul of a pea," she says. "How else can I explain that you would think of trading something so priceless for money?" Her voice takes on a self-congratulatory tone. "What I have done is far more profound. I have broken with the past and provided for the future of the letters." Then on a note of triumph, Mme Colmar exclaims, "I have given them to François!" She takes my arm again. "It is all legal. *He* and only he now owns the letters. You shall never see them."

Berthe stares at her mother, mouth ajar, her small agate eyes incredulous. The bluish crescents under her eyes seem darker. "You are mad. An old fool. Worse than Papa. At least he is harmless." For a moment I have the impression that she is about to strike her mother. "You have given away something that has been in our family for three hundred years. More than that. You have given away my patrimony. Something rightfully mine. I counted on those letters to support the burden of my old age. So I do not become like you, and live like this." She waves a hand at the surrounding walls. "You have given away my future. And to someone whose only merit is that he satisfies you in bed. What lunacy possessed you?" Mme Colmar lets go of me, her eyes waver. I can see that her anger has passed. After all, she didn't die the other night as she thought she would. "You have given away something of incalculable value... to our family, to France." Mme Colmar is now looking down, like a scolded child. Berthe turns to me. "Where are the letters?"

"I no longer have them."

"What do you mean?" Berthe says. "What have you

done with them?" Mme Colmar has raised her eyes and now both she and her daughter are staring at me.

"I gave them to a friend for safekeeping," I say.

"Why would you part with them?" Mme Colmar asks. "They were safe where they were. Why did you take them out of this house?" She continues to stare at me, her face perplexed, as though trying to place someone she has once known but now only vaguely recognizes. I do not answer. Then Mme Colmar's eyes narrow. "What friend?" she asks, her voice now resembling her daughter's. I still don't answer. "Is it the girl who was here?" Her eyes are now bright in their hollows.

I can't bring myself to say yes and look away.

Mme Colmar lets out a scream, a loud wailing "Ahhh!" and a shiver of fright and guilt runs through me. "What have you done?" Madame's voice now rises in pitch. "That girl is a whore! Worse. She's a charlatan. A fraud."

"Wait," Berthe says. "Let us go to your friend's home. Now. This moment."

"She's at school this morning."

"Then let us find her at school."

As we leave I turn to Mme Colmar. Her look is now unfocused, befuddled. Lines, like the broken wings of a bird, sag down from her nose to the edges of her mouth. Her eyes seem faded. She suddenly appears absolutely ancient. What have I done? I want to apologize but know that words no longer matter. I feel a lump in my throat. I pray that Lea is at school, or in her apartment, but have a suspicion that Lea will not be in any of these places.

"Mademoiselle Mervaud has left," says the flat-chested concierge after our visit to her classes at the Sorbonne failed to turn up Lea.

"What do you mean 'left?'" I ask, having difficulty with the obvious.

"She has gone," says the concierge impatiently. "With her baggage. The apartment is vacant."

"Did she say where she was going?"

The woman shrugs. "They never say where they are going."

I check the Crédit Lyonnais in the Place Maubert. They never heard of Lea Mervaud.

Mme Colmar comes into my room, her hair down and in disorder. Her eyes are cast toward the floor and I have never seen her back hunched over this way. "My body is bent because nothing is left to hold it erect," she says as though she has read my mind, and takes the chair beside my desk. The old man wanders in and stands behind his wife. They suddenly look alike.

"My daughter wished to go to the police," Madame says, "but I dissuaded her. The letters, after all, are legitimately yours, to dispose of as you will. Besides, why expose to the world the folly of a muddled old woman?" She gazes at the floorboards. "I should have died when I thought I would. Leaped from the Eiffel Tower if I had to. Taken poison. Drowned in the Seine... Now I have nothing. Not my letters, not my books, not my clothes, not even the pots and pans in my kitchen." The bitterness in Madame's voice and face is of one abandoned, forsaken by Providence to suffer a final indignity.

We stay this way, all staring at the floor, a tableau in sadness while I'm trying to think of something I could possibly say. It occurs to me, like a foreshadowing of horrors to come, that my pursuit of the letters, from covert greed to outright lust, was the first instance of obsession in my life.

Mme Colmar finally lifts her eyes. "How is it possible," she asks, "that within days after I gave you the letters they were gone?"

I suppose I could have kept the truth from her, trumped up some excuse. Instead I sigh, a heavy indrawing and expulsion of breath, then say in a flat voice, "I stole them. I removed them from the safe before you gave them to me." I feel better as soon as I say this; Mme Colmar looks more awful yet.

"You did what?" she asks.

"I took them," I repeat. "A week before your gift. When I believed you would soon die and it would no longer matter."

"But they were not yours," Madame says. Then her look slowly shifts; first it is of confusion, then of deepest wretchedness. "What did you hope to obtain?"

I look away—to the Daumier print of the sly attorney and his disreputable client. "Money," I say. "The money to remain in Paris."

Madame stares at me. "Ohhh," she says, the sound a soft moan, distant and ghost-like. I think of the death of Laurent. "I misjudged you completely."

"I'm so sorry," I mumble. It's all I can manage.

"You were corruptible and were corrupted by that whore. She persuaded you to commit the most terrible of crimes, to betray someone who trusted you. Trusted you absolutely. She convinced you to sneak around my house, a thief in the night, and steal something I had openly revealed and shared with you. And you, morally weak, did not have the strength to resist."

"I'm so terribly sorry," I repeat, though I know it's useless.

Madame nods up and down slowly and her eyes blur. "This will weigh like a curse upon your head until the day that you die." A tear rolls down one cheek then the other. I wish that I were dead. Her tears are the most terrible thing; I move to comfort her but she pulls away. "Now none of us has the letters," she says. "Not you, not I, not Berthe. Now it is your whore who possesses the legacy of my family." She gazes at me, tears streaked around her mouth, her face in ruins. "You must leave," she says in a barely audible voice then looks at the floorboards again and is silent.

"I might as well go now," I say, though I have no idea where to go. I dump my drip-dry clothing, dirty laundry, notebooks, and, on impulse, Madame's journal, into my B-4 bag. To my surprise I feel the wetness of my own tears on my cheeks as I do this.

Madame finally looks up and watches me cry, her face expressionless. "Let me hold you for the last time," I say. She slowly rises and stands beside my desk, now perfectly erect, staring downward. I hold her close but her arms hang at her sides. "Poor weak François," she says. Her body has stiffened as though I'm a stranger. M. Colmar wanders over to the window and heaves it open. A pleasant spring breeze enters the room.

16

I am now almost
as old as Mme Colmar was when I roomed in her apartment on the Rue Danton.

I had not thought of Madame for years until an incident that occurred about six months ago. A banker friend, a certain Victor Cobb, who also arranged the purchase of the town house where I live, on a narrow tree-lined street near Louisburg Square in Boston's Beacon Hill, invited me to a cocktail party. I arrived with a friend, a twenty-five year old brunette named Jennifer. (I introduce these young women as "friends." What other polite name is there? We do indeed speak a little: I listen to their trivial woes, soothe their hurts by stroking their lithe bodies as we lie in my bed, shades drawn, a dim lamp in the corner, drinking Tanqueray martinis. Like King David, I need them to warm my old bones.) Two young men asked Jennifer what bank she was with. She nodded in my direction and the men laughed. I

187

didn't mind; I found it amusing as well.

I noticed a slender grey-haired woman, not unattractive, sitting alone in the corner of a couch, stirring a cup of coffee on the table in front of her, and experienced an uneasy sense of recognition. As I tried to solve the puzzle of her identity (my fear was that I had met her only the week before), she looked directly at me and smiled. I excused myself, worked my way around a clump of men, and stood before the woman. "My name is Frank Reeber," I said.

"That's what I thought," she replied. "I'm Lea Hayes, but you would know me as Lea Mervaud. Do sit down. Tell me about your life... Was it any good? Were you an inspiration, like the Leech-gatherer on the lonely moor?" I located an empty chair and pulled it over so that I sat facing her, my martini glass on the coffee table between us. The woman's face was broad, strong-jawed, forward-thrusting, giving her an anguine appearance, an effect accentuated by her wide mouth and green eyes. Yet the crevasses that fell away from her nose and mouth created a vulnerable expression at variance with the rest of her face. As she waited for my answer, she cocked her head and elevated an eyebrow and I recognized her then. It was indeed Lea.

"What happened to the letters?" I asked. She stared at me uncomprehending. "The Sévigné letters," I prompted. "You bailed out on me in Paris, a million years ago... remember? When I asked you to return the letters. I've always considered that one of the great betrayals of my life." I thought overkill was definitely in order. "It changed forever the way I looked at people. After that, I never completely trusted anyone."

Lea's brow wrinkled and her expression grew mournful. "Why you poor man," she said. "You've spent a lifetime making something of nothing." She made a small gesture then let her hand fall on the purse beside her. "Now I recall those silly letters. They may have had some sentimental value but they weren't worth much in the way of money. I remember that after a great deal of effort, I sold the whole lot for something around fifteen hundred dollars." I found this impossible to believe, for in my mind the value of the letters equated to at least the Kohinoor diamond. I studied Lea's face; she seemed to be telling the truth but I couldn't put much faith in that. Certainly her lack of recollection of the letters a minute ago had seemed genuine enough; besides, why would she lie forty-two years after the fact? "Don't ask me where the money went," she said. "It disappeared the way all money disappears."

"I looked for you when I returned to the U.S.," I said. "To find out what happened to the letters. Your parents told me you'd stayed in France. They offered to give me your address, but then I figured since you'd snuck away, writing wouldn't make any difference."

Lea took a sip of her coffee. If she was stricken with remorse, or for that matter experienced any regret at all, I couldn't find it. "I married a Frenchman," Lea said, as though by way of explanation. "When I met him, he'd just inherited the family business, a building materials company, from his father who'd been killed in an automobile accident." I sensed life history in the air and leaned back, finished my martini. I could see there would be no further talk about the letters. "The man had a delightful name, Florian, and a face to match. I got him to propose to me in three weeks. I should have recognized this as a danger sign, the action of a man given to sudden enthusiasms, instead of attributing it to my charm. In the next two years he frittered away his inheritance on all sorts of fanciful ventures: a hatchery for tropical fish, natural gas exploration in the Sahara, orchid growing, importing Persian cats, and I don't remember what else. The man had a unique gift for investing in crazy things and there was no talking him out of it. I ran the building materials business but it was

189

impossible to keep up with the drain of his investments. Florian was really a poet at heart, spent long hours staring at the moon and the new-fallen snow, wrote wistful little verses, quoted Paul Eluard."

Lea seemed genuinely touched by the recollection of her husband, but I had barely listened. I was stuck on something else—the revelation that the Sévigné letters hadn't been worth much after all. I remembered that Mme Colmar's daughter, whose name at that moment I could not recall, was counting on the letters to lighten the burden of her old age and her bitter lament that her mother had given away her future. Why it had all been an illusion!

I felt a hand on my shoulder; Victor Cobb was offering me a second martini; I thanked him and nodded yes.

Lea then went on to recount the story of her second marriage, to an executive at Michelin, who showed great promise but also turned out to be a dud, and her miserable life in Clermont-Ferrand. I didn't listen to that either. Instead I recalled, like images from a movie seen in childhood, Mme Colmar extending the brass container toward me, fleur-de-lis engraved on the cover, a tawny gold sarcophagus; inside the grey-brown papers, covered with orderly looping characters, lay like artifacts of an ancient civilization. The shade of Mme Colmar hovered over me. *"What were they really?"* I asked Madame's ghost. *"Ah,* chéri,*" she replied, her face surprisingly youthful and gay, "the letters were but a mirror reflecting everyone's desire: a safe haven for my daughter, the means for you to hold onto Paris a while longer, and a source of wealth for your whore."*

"I was right about some things, wrong about a lot of others," Lea was saying, then went on to elaborate the rights and wrongs of her second marriage. Her French accent was stronger than I remembered.

"It's difficult to believe this putain was right about

anything," said the specter of Mme Colmar.

"I will tell you one thing she was right about," I said. "She believed life without money was neither pleasant nor romantic. I have come to agree with her. And I believe you would as well. I look back on my attempt at writing as a ridiculous fantasy, more an excuse to escape responsibility than anything serious."

"What did you do when you returned to America?" Madame asked, the suggestion of a frown on her face.

"I worked as an engineer. Then one day—a rainy day as I recall, as I was completing the design of a rather clever circuit—it dawned on me that working for others was a poor investment of my time. Success in working for others made others rich while I received only a small part of the gain. The road to wealth, I concluded, was through the investment of my sweat and such money as I could scrape together in my own enterprise. There high risk could result in high reward, and success depended only on my judgement, undiluted by the judgement of others. 'Better to be first in the village than second in Rome,' I told my wife as I invested every dollar we had in a new business and took another mortgage on our house. 'Milton said it better,' she observed. 'Better to reign in hell than serve in heaven.'"

"Did all this make you happy?" Madame asked. She seemed truly interested.

"No, not in the least. It gave me satisfaction but never brought happiness. I worked nights, weekends. The business prospered but my family was destroyed. I married once again and divorced again. I have five children, two sons and three daughters. The older boy helps me run the business; the younger one is worthless. He and the girls are scattered around the northeast of America, together with my eight grandchildren."

"But all that is in the past and unchangeable, my poor François," Madame said. "What occupies you now?"

191

"Death occupies me. The fear of death, which never afflicted me when I was young, now surfaces almost every day. Usually toward evening as I sit in my office and stare at the papers on my desk. I sometimes gaze at my hands and imagine the bones underneath exposed and dry; at that moment I grow dizzy, as though the floor were tilting, and I become aware of my own heartbeat. Other times I visualize my own grave, set in a vastness of headstones, indistinguishable from the rest, and on it is written, Franklin Reeber, born November 15, 1925, died such-and-such a date, then the inscription 'It all passed in the blink of an eye.'"

Madame shrugged. She did not appear sympathetic. "Every man must come to terms with his own death," she said.

"Here I've been babbling about myself," Lea said, "and never gave you a chance to answer my question. Tell me, then, did you have a good life?"

How do you answer a question like that? "It's hard to say," I said, not exactly ablaze with insight. "It all went by like some long airline flight. You try to do some work, eat, lust after the stewardesses, watch the movie, nap, then when you look back you find the trip took no time at all. If I had to do it over again, I'd try harder not to make a mess of my marriage and family."

"That's not much of an answer," Lea laughed. "I thought I would hear the Rime of the Ancient Mariner. Well then, let me tell you something about my third husband." I had the impression that the story of her life had become the most important thing in her life and she was bent on telling it no matter what.

I regarded the woman who had instigated my great moral crisis: she was more slender than I remembered, something coiled, cobra-like about her; her laugh had revealed her eye teeth, darker than the rest. Poisonous fangs. To think she had been so important to me! Even chased her across an ocean. She had persuaded me to write and persuaded me to steal. And I a willing accomplice. How altogether extraordinary.

Lea raised her cup then set it down. "Frank," she said, "—I think we know each other well enough for me to call you by your first name—would you be kind enough to get me another cup of coffee?"

I took the cup, passed Jennifer who was with another group of bankers, and went to the kitchen where, amidst a welter of glasses and plates, I set the cup down. I then looked around, at the jumble of silverware, dishes and liquor bottles, the stove, refrigerator and dishwasher, and experienced first a rising sense of confusion then the familiar panic. Why was I there? I looked about me again and felt dampness erupt on my forehead. Why was I in this room? I decided, as I usually do in this circumstance, to retrace my steps; I left the kitchen and was met by Victor Cobb. "I'd like you to meet—" then he stopped. "Are you all right?"

"I'm fine," I said, and brushed past him and found Lea. "I'm sorry," I said, "I must have been asleep at the switch. What was it that you asked for?"

Lea regarded me for an instant. "A cup of coffee. Black. I have cream here." I was about to leave when she added, "And please bring a spoon." I looked at the table: there was a napkin with a damp stain next to the cream pitcher. "You took the other spoon with you when you took the coffee cup," she said.

I repeated the words coffee and spoon to myself as I went back to the kitchen and returned with a cup of black coffee and a spoon, once again brushed aside Cobb, and set them before Lea. I watched her add cream and stir the coffee. "My third husband is an American, a Boston banker named Peter Hayes. It was the third marriage for both of us and we were grateful to have found each other. At some point, though, a strange thing happened. I began to feel that I was someone else, a certain French writer. It came over me at odd moments and wasn't make believe. I felt that I truly was that person. I would ask Peter to call me by her name, at first as a lark, but later I would answer only to her name. I dressed like her. I insisted that Peter buy me a sports car like hers—it was a Triumph, a TR-3. I guess it was a bizarre form of mid-life crisis, but I *became* that person."

I looked at the two empty martini glasses on the coffee table. Maybe it was Cobb's lousy liquor, I thought. The son of a bitch always skimped on booze.

"You don't really believe it's the liquor, do you?" the wraith of Mme Colmar asked.

"No, you're right, it's not the liquor," I said. "These episodes occur quite often now. At work I have become a man perpetually coming into the middle of a film, forgetting decisions already taken, plans already made. At meetings I often see a patient expression on the faces around me and know that I'm repeating myself. When things go badly, I become red-faced and bursting with anger. I shout in people's faces. My son says that I overreact, that I'm obsessed with trivia. He has an important degree, a master's in Business Administration from Harvard University. But instead of worrying about our products and our customers, he's concerned with such high-minded merde *as strategic planning, optimal organization, government business policy. 'Issue' is a large word in his vocabulary. Whenever we disagree he says we have an 'issue'—it seems so harmless, so chaste, when he uses the word I imagine a wedge of angel food cake lying on a plate. He urges me to retire, tells me, his face full of sincerity, 'You've earned it.' More* merde. *Sometimes he tactfully suggests that I sell the business."*

"What do the other children say?"

"The others are more direct. 'Sell the cursed thing,' they

say. 'It only makes you miserable. Buy an estate in Florida. Enjoy yourself.' All merde. *I'm certain my son is talking to them, telling them that I'm disrupting things, that I've upset good people and caused them to leave. The children must think I'm falling apart and want me to sell before I bring the place to ruin. When I die they will sell. I have no doubt they'll squander the money, without any thought of what it took to make it. Why, I ask you, would I want to sell this thing that for me is more precious than diamonds? No, to hell with them all, I and the business shall sink together. I sleep badly, experience ringing in my ears, can't concentrate, overhear conversations where I'm ridiculed. But I'm going to cling to this precious thing until I die."*

"Peter was clearly worried. He couldn't take me to his business affairs because I insisted I was someone else. He suggested psychoanalysis which I considered absurd. I spoke of my new book that was about to be published. In answer to his criticism, I pointed out that I was far too busy to worry about the house. I had my editor to contend with who was always trying to modify my material. Peter finally had me committed to an expensive psychiatric hospital outside of Stamford, Connecticut. There was therapy of various kinds which I hardly remember. I came out of it slowly. There were times when I was still the writer, but they were further apart. Finally I was back to being just plain Lea."

As Lea spoke, my eye was caught by glints of light reflected from her coffee spoon as she toyed with it. The spoon was an odd size: smaller than a teaspoon, larger than a demi-tasse. It was of silver and there was an intricate pattern of leaves on the handle. She had finished her coffee and wiped the spoon on the napkin and now her fingers caressed the pattern, slowly and gently moving the thumb and forefinger of her right hand across the silver undulations.

Someone touched my shoulder. It was Victor Cobb again. "Frank, I would like you to meet Peter Hayes."

I shook hands with a chunky grey-haired man whom I judged some years younger than I. "I notice that you and my wife have had quite a conversation," Hayes said.

"We helped each other through a difficult time, long ago," I said. I turned to Lea who was snapping her purse shut. The coffee spoon was gone.

"Can I get you another drink?" Cobb asked. I shook my head as Hayes started to describe an approach to corporate capital formation that his bank had pioneered.

"Why don't you drive," I said to Jennifer.

"Who was that old lady you spent the whole evening with?" she asked as she happily slipped behind the wheel of my Mercedes.

"Somebody I knew in another life."

I returned to the letters and the ghost of Mme Colmar. She now wore her impish smile. *"I expected better of you,* chéri," *she said. "You, like the others, valued the letters incorrectly. They were but symbols—symbols that connected me to my ancestors, to the past grandeur of France— and like all symbols they had value in your mind and not in your purse. The letters provided continuity to my life and could have done the same for yours. Like memory itself, they were beyond price."*

Jennifer drove east on Route 9, past the Chestnut Hill mall as Madame, her face relaxed and lovely, continued. *"The betrayal by your whore did not surprise me and surely could not have surprised you. But your betrayal, dear François, was an altogether different matter. It demonstrated that my judgement of your character, the intuitive, instinctive judgement on which I relied so completely and which caused me to will the precious legacy of my family to you, was wrong. It was more than the letters that you destroyed. You put an end to me. Surely you are subtle enough to understand this. In your heart,* chéri, *you never believed that my death was tied to Mme de Sévigné. But then you yourself proved that my belief was not altogether false. By stealing the letters you cut me off from the past that nurtured me. My life could not long continue after that."*

Madame was silent for a moment. "Did you ever think of me when you returned to America?"

"In the beginning yes. I even considered making amends. Sending money. If not to you then at least to your daughter. But in the press of other activities, a world away, it all grew unreal, as though the incident had never occurred, and it faded from my mind."

"Then you were not changed at all by the crime you committed?" Madame asked, her face incredulous.

"Oh, but yes!" I exclaimed. "I was changed. Changed terribly. For some events, crucial actions in your life, never really leave you, they reverberate through time and change you forever, whether you think of them or not. And so it was with the theft of your letters. Do you recall saying that the event would weigh like a curse upon my head? It did indeed, whether I was conscious of it or not. For the anxiety that you suffered attached itself to me. I was always afraid of failure, worked like a dog to avoid it, and in the process destroyed two marriages and never knew my own children. The theft also left a residue of shame in me, a stigmata of worthlessness that only I could perceive. I never felt myself deserving of the success I achieved or what little love was offered me. And so I spent my life anxious, restless, sometimes desperate, always driven, branded by a perfidy I had committed when I was only twenty-five but that could never be eradicated."

"But that is only proper," Madame said, turning her hands palms up before her. "Some things can never be undone."

197

*"I now think of you with great tenderness," I said,
feeling myself overflowing with tenderness. "I was always
astonished at how intensely you savored the few crumbs
that life offered you. At a concert, the cinema, or reading
poetry to me, I could not believe that you were moved to
tears. It never failed to surprise me—how active a partici-
pant you were."*

*"But there is no boundary that divides these experiences
from life,"* Mme Colmar *said, her eyes crinkling with
amusement.*

*"I suppose that the way we love is the most revealing
thing about us, and you,* ma chère Madame, *at the age of
seventy, were as passionate as a schoolgirl... Do you
remember the long winter evenings, the world darkening
around us, when we walked the streets of Paris, arms
around each other's waist?"*

"Of course I remember."

*"I recall those moments now as the most perfect of my
life. The streets were illuminated by gas lamps and as the
dusk wore on their fire gathered in pools of brightness on
the pavement and shone on your beautiful face... I will now
tell you something that I have just discovered, this very
minute, in an epiphany of recognition that makes it difficult
for me to speak. For a brief time, long ago,* ma chère
Madame, ma chère Honorine, *I loved you, deeply and
perfectly."*

"How sweet of you to say that, chéri. *But do not
reminisce. It is bad to reminisce... Did you ever return to
Paris?"*

*"On business, perhaps half a dozen times. At each visit
I saw the city changing. I saw the air turn yellow-brown.
The tower of Montparnasse blight the loveliest*
arrondissement. *The high-rise offices of the Défense hem in
and trivialize the city. Les Halles gone. Fast food empori-
ums replace the cafes. Graffiti mar the walls. The* putains

who once lounged on street corners, their wares clearly on display, roam the boulevards in convertible automobiles. Centuries of blackening, like accreted experience, removed from the façades of buildings, revealing a naked whiteness underneath, dark beauty obliterated. With each visit the city became increasingly a stranger."

"Did you ever return to the Rue Danton?"

"No... I thought of doing that but always decided against it. I knew it would seem small, run down, disappointing. Then I didn't want to relive that April day when I packed my old army bag, hugged you for the last time (the body of a stranger!), and fled into the streets where all things—houses and avenues, trees and people—stared, hostile and accusing, at my tear-streaked face."

Of the gifts Madame gave me, all were lost except for one, the silver bracelet with the name François engraved on it. It lies at the bottom of a drawer, never worn, black with tarnish. I located the oversized green-covered notebook under a stack of old income tax records in a cardboard box that had traveled from garage to garage and now moldered in a basement storage cabinet. The book resembled an accountant's ledger or a laboratory notebook. I opened Mme Colmar's journal for the first time the day after my encounter with Lea at Cobb's cocktail party. Her script was surprisingly large, the letters rounded, feminine, easy to read, all writing square with the page though the paper was unlined. (I also found, under Madame's journal, the novel I had worked on in Paris, the pages smelling of mildew. I waited a month before opening it, then, touched by the juvenile handwriting, read the manuscript in a single evening. I was astonished at how good some of it was and dismayed by the self-pitying drivel in the rest of it.)

Lapses of memory now occur more frequently. I imagine a defect in the machinery that weaves the fabric of my memory, a defect that will progressively worsen until events cease to exist the instant after they occur. Then the fabric itself, which forms my entire life, all that I have experienced, suffered, won and lost, will rupture, strand by precious strand, until I am left a confused hulk, with no past and a present that moment by moment disappears into a void. Since the conversation with Lea, that image now alternates with another: a picture of the lost old man in his seedy bathrobe wandering around the apartment on the Rue Danton, flinging open windows. *I will become Monsieur Colmar.* Then panic grips my throat and I feel a burst of dampness on my forehead.

"How interesting to see you writing," Madame says to me. *"I notice you are using the same composition notebook, the one with the mottled black and white cover, as you did in Paris. What are you writing now?"*

"I'm writing my memoirs," I say.

"Always the autobiographer. For whose benefit are you doing this?"

"For my children and my grandchildren. I want them to better understand their father, their grandfather, and what he did... To learn from my experience."

"How very touching. And naive. One does not learn from another's experience. Isn't that the essence of experience? That it happens to you and not to another? How do you transfer that?... You were always willing to settle for shallow answers, cher François. *Consider further. Why are you sitting there, a bald old man, wearing half-moon glasses, bent over a child's notebook, scribbling once again?"*

I think about this. "I write, I suppose, for the same reason that you kept your journal. Because I want to hold onto my memory, to press back the encroaching darkness... to make sense of my life."

"*And what have you concluded?*"

I think a while longer. "*That I have truly lived and achieved only when I allowed myself to be ruled by passion, when I swept away reason and became passion's slave.*"

Madame nods, makes a small gesture with her hands. "*A modest conclusion but better than none at all.*" *She contemplates my face.* "*I notice you have kept your mustache,*" *she says, apparently bored with the lessons of my life.* "*You should do a better job of trimming it. You resemble a sorrowful Maréchal Pétain.*"

As I write, Mme Colmar drifts in and out of the room. Sometimes she sits in the chair beside my desk and we chat. "*I know that after I die the children will sell the business,*" *I said to her the other day.* "*But I desperately hope that they will not. Perhaps I have started something and after I am gone they will all come together and make it flourish and grow. Maybe I have begun something that, like your Sévigné letters, will endure for generations.*"

"*It's comforting to think so,*" *Madame replied.*

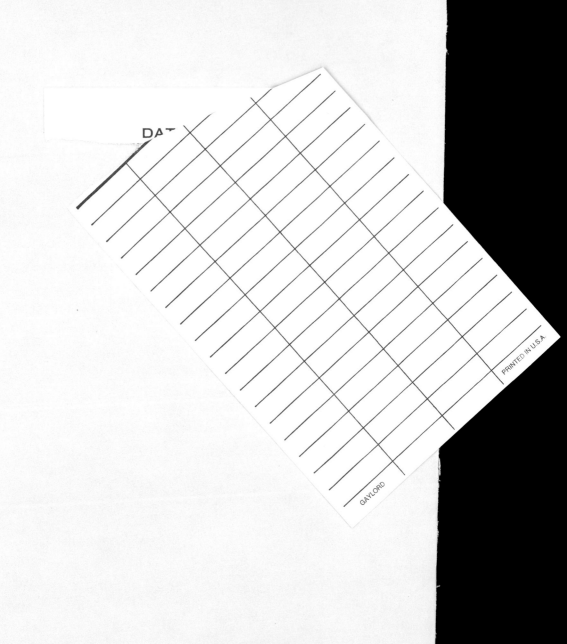

DAT

GAYLORD

PRINTED IN U.S.A.